Necessary Noise

stories about our families
as they really are

Necessary Noise
stories about our families as they really are

EDITED BY
MICHAEL CART

ILLUSTRATIONS BY CHARLOTTE NORUZI

JOANNA COTLER BOOKS

An Imprint of HarperCollinsPublishers

Necessary Noise: Stories About Our Families as They Really Are

"Hardware" copyright © 2003 by Joan Bauer

"Siskiyou Sloan and the Eye of the Giraffe" copyright © 2003 by Norma Howe

"Necessary Noise" copyright © 2003 by Emma Donoghue

"The Throwaway: A Suite" copyright © 2003 by Nikki Grimes

"Visit" copyright © 2003 by Walter Dean Myers

"A Family Illness: A Mom-Son Conversation" copyright © 2003 by Joyce Carol Thomas

"A Woman's Touch" copyright © 2003 by Rita Williams-Garcia

"Sailing Away" copyright © 2003 by Michael Cart

"Dr. Jekyll and Sister Hyde" copyright © 2003 by Sonya Sones

"Snowbound" copyright © 2003 by Lois Lowry

Copyright © 2003 by Michael Cart

www.harpertempest.com

Library of Congress Cataloging-in-Publication Data

Necessary noise : stories about our families as they really are / edited by Michael Cart ; illustrations by Charlotte Noruzi.— 1st ed.

v. cm.

"Joanna Cotler Books."

Contents: Hardware / Joan Bauer — Siskiyou Sloan and the eye of the giraffe / Norma Howe — Necessary noise / Emma Donoghue — The throwaway / Nikki Grimes — Visit / Walter Dean Myers — A family illness / Joyce Carol Thomas — A woman's touch / Rita Williams-Garcia — Sailing away / Michael Cart — Dr. Jekyll and Sister Hyde / Sonya Sones — Snowbound / Lois Lowry.

ISBN 0-06-027499-9 — ISBN 0-06-027500-6 (lib. bdg.)

1. Family—Juvenile fiction. 2. Young adult fiction, American. [1. Family—Fiction. 2. Short stories.] I. Cart, Michael. II. Noruzi, Charlotte, ill.

PZ5 .N26 2003   2002151058

[Fic]—dc21

Typography by Alicia Mikles

1   2   3   4   5   6   7   8   9   10

❖

First Edition

For William C. Morris
with friendship and gratitude for his countless contributions
to the world of books for young readers
—M.C.

CONTENTS

INTRODUCTION

People of my generation (I'm sixty-one) grew up in the fifties in traditional nuclear families. They were functional (or so we liked to think) units that consisted of a father, a mother (married, of course), and two children (ideally a boy and a girl). Dad was the breadwinner and Mom was the homemaker. It was an *Ozzie and Harriet, Father Knows Best, Leave It to Beaver* kind of world. (But did Mom really wear pearls and high heels to vacuum?) The dictionary defined *family* as a fundamental group in society typically consisting of a man and woman and their offspring. In fact, that could have described fully 45 percent of American households well into the 1970s.

But times change. And today a mere 24 percent of U.S. households are "married with children." So what does that word *family* mean to teenagers today?

Well, consider the following: Americans are now less likely to marry than at any time in our nation's history. A total of 32 percent of adult Americans are unmarried and childless. Twelve percent are unmarried but have children. The remaining 56 percent—those who do marry—are divorcing in near record numbers (almost 50 percent of marriages now end in divorce, compared to 30 percent as recently as 1970).

As a result, more than half of America's young people now grow up in single-parent households; 24 percent of children live in mother-only households, while 2 percent live with their fathers (the number of single-father households rose a dramatic 62 percent in the 1990s); others are being raised by older siblings or by grandparents (or by a single grandparent). Still others turn to peers or to gangs to provide a surrogate experience of family love and support. No wonder that the once-upon-a-time nuclear family is now routinely described as "fractured," "blended," "at risk," and "in transition."

Other factors also contribute to these seismic changes. The exponential increase in immigration from nonwestern countries has brought new cultures with their own "new" definitions of family to America. Meanwhile, the gay rights movement has given rise to another kind of family: one headed by same-sex parents or by a single gay or lesbian parent.

Combine these social factors with economic forces and you find that families now also constitute 40 percent of the homeless population (young people under eighteen comprise 25 percent). Worse, nearly three fourths of children in single-parent families will experience poverty by age eleven.

How can kids who are living outside the mainstream in radically nontraditional families deal with their circum-stances—circumstances that often result in their being marginalized, rendered invisible, regarded as unacceptably different, or even being persecuted by peers? And how, too, can mainstream kids begin to comprehend—intellectually and emotionally—the dramatic differences that now define the daily lives of so many "other" teens? How can they learn empathy? How, in short, can "other" become "us"?

One way, I think, is through reading fiction that captures—artfully, authentically, and unsparingly—the circumstances of kids whose lives are a daily experience of redefining *family*. And that is why I invited nine leading writers for young adults to consider the question "What does the word *family* mean to teenagers today?" (I've contributed a tenth story of my own.) Their answers are as individual as American households in the twenty-first century are. Consider:

Joan Bauer's funny and heartfelt story "Hardware" examines the struggle of Cali's factionalized and fractionalized family to save its hardware store when a megadiscount emporium moves in across the street. In the process, Cali discovers that in shared adversity a community can become a kind of family, too.

Norma Howe's wonderfully offbeat "Siskiyou Sloan and the Eye of the Giraffe" is the story of a brother and sister whose lives have been defined by their radically differing views of the world: skepticism and belief, respectively. Those views will be tested when the family dog dies and a long-lost toy giraffe magically reappears—or does it?

Emma Donoghue's "Necessary Noise" is also a story about siblings, a brilliantly reimagined contemporary telling of the biblical tale of the sisters Mary and Martha and their brother, Lazarus. When their younger brother overdoses on drugs, two sisters talk with increasing passion about their difficult family circumstances and, by making this "necessary noise," take cautious first steps toward healing.

Nikki Grimes's elegant story in verse, "The Throwaway: A Suite," also finds inspiration in a biblical story—that of Ishmael and his mother, Hagar, who shared the plight of many contemporary single-parent families: homelessness and abandonment. It also reminds us that even in the ancient world, family was providing theme and inspiration for story-tellers.

Walter Dean Myers's "Visit" is a breathtakingly powerful story of a father's first visit to his son in twenty years, a visit that takes place on death row. As the two converse in spare, understated language, themes of abandonment and parental guilt emerge, climaxing in a harrowing final scene that no reader will forget.

Joyce Carol Thomas's "A Family Illness" is another parent-son story, but this time the parent is the mother whose dialogue with her son reveals, with a powerful emotional resonance, his battle against mental illness, which he hauntingly describes as "living in a circle of tigers."

Rita Williams-Garcia's "A Woman's Touch" is a story about a boy with two mothers—his biological mom and her lesbian lover. Desperately missing his father, the boy resents his mother's new partner and wonders who will teach him to be a man. The answer he discovers may surprise you.

My own story, "Sailing Away," examines the lifelong friendship of two boys who, following a death in one of their families, become surrogate brothers and then something more.

Sonya Sones's "Dr. Jekyll and Sister Hyde" is a beautifully realized story in verse. At once harrowing, humorous, and heartfelt, it examines the dramatically dysfunctional relationship of two sisters and their clueless parents.

Lois Lowry's "Snowbound" is the hilarious story of the invasion of a traditional family one snowy winter weekend by the college-age daughter and her obnoxious boyfriend, Loosh (short for Lucien), who sleeps in the nude and refuses to eat what he contentiously calls "mammal."

Though many of the stories in this collection are dark in tone and challenging in thematic intensity, the stories that begin and end it—"Hardware" and "Snowbound"—are salutary reminders that family life, however it is defined today, still offers latitude for light and healing laughter.

Finally, these ten stories—whether light or dark in their depiction of families that may be whole or fractured, functional or dysfunctional, traditional or in radical transition—remind us, too, of the abiding importance of dialogue, of discussion, of talking about our circumstances, of leaving room, in short, for some necessary noise.

Necessary Noise

stories about our families
as they really are

Hardware

BY JOAN BAUER

They tried to drag Aunt Phil from the street.

It shouldn't have been that hard.

To begin with she isn't too big.

Five foot four to be exact.

She isn't that young either.

Fifty-three as of last Tuesday.

But she was angry and she had a hammer.

The brand she'd just put on sale for $9.99. And she was raising that tool, spitting fury at a huge hole in the ground one block long; shrieking at a four-story gargantuan plastic Waldo head that was being erected right before her eyes.

Cali tried gently but firmly to get her inside, but there's just so much a teenager can do against an aunt with a hammer.

Lewis, Cali's half cousin, tried to help, but he always made things worse. "Everyone's looking at you, Phil. You want them to think you're *crazy?*"

Aunt Phil turned to him with half-crazy eyes. "The world's gone mad, Mr. Insight. Not me." She looked at Cali. "Am I right?"

Cali half squirmed. "Sort of, Aunt Phil. You're sort of right."

Aunt Phil had always been a fighter.

When the mayor had proposed a zoning tax on small businesses, Aunt Phil took to the streets, screaming that small business owners were going to fight back and defend their stores "with our bare feet if necessary."

"That's bare hands, Aunt Phil," Cali had whispered.

"Whatever." Phil stood tough.

When two shoplifters tried to rob her store blind, Phil cornered them with her turbocharged staple gun.

"Drop the merchandise, scumbags, or I'll staple your nostrils together."

Big Mel, Cali's partial uncle, called the police, who hauled those terrified thieves off to jail.

"You plot against the innocent, you pay!" Phil screamed, waving her staple gun.

"You're not innocent, lady!" one of the robbers shouted back.

But as Big Mel always said, "You never know what's going to make the glass run over. You never know what's going to split the last straw down the backside."

And what it was for Aunt Phil and Cali's family and Phil's Hardware Store and all the little family-run stores on Lattice Avenue was Waldo's SuperStore moving in across the street. One block long.

They had everything.

Groceries.

Hardware.

Paint.

Clothes.

Whatever a human being needed, Waldo's had it.

At discount prices.

No small store could survive when a Waldo's came to town.

Aunt Phil raised an angry fist at the Waldo's truck as it rumbled by.

"You think you can just move in here with your big muck trucks and tear out my heart in public? You think God is not going to judge you for putting up your establishment right across from where my father, may God rest his soul, built this store brick by brick by the sweat of his person?"

Cali cleared her throat to keep Phil honest. The store wasn't made of brick and Aunt Phil's father, Andrew, who was Cali's great-uncle, paid his sister's second husband, Wilfred, to build it.

"This is sacred ground, you morons!"

Store owners on Lattice Avenue were coming outside to see what all the racket was about.

Lester Malloy from Lester's Grill.

Mrs. Caselli from the bakery.

Mr. and Mrs. Toole from AAA Extermination and their no-good son, Weston.

They stood there and let her rail, like a family with a crazy relative who no one can keep quiet.

When you've been through what these store owners had been through, everyone on the street was like family.

Weston scratched his stomach and half leered at Cali. Cali always suspected that AAA Extermination's key weapon against rats was Weston. One look at Weston and any self-respecting rat would run for cover.

Phil put her hammer down. A good sign.

Lewis moved closer. Gently picked up the hammer.

Aunt Phil let Cali guide her inside. When a person has

spent thirty minutes screaming at morons, it takes a lot out of you.

Big Mel had finished four glazed doughnuts, almost without chewing. He sloshed the coffee in his mug, took a slurp, and said, "Look, we can't fight it. Waldo's has offered us not much to sell the store, but it's either that or die, slowly bleeding in the street."

Big Mel was Aunt Phil's half brother.

Most relationships in Cali's family were explained by fractions.

"I don't bleed in public," Phil announced, whose role in the family was to dispute whatever Big Mel said.

"We're not going to get anywhere this way," Cali's mother said. Cali's mother's role in the family was to try to help people be reasonable. It was a lonely job.

"He's happy to sell out to pirates!" Aunt Phil screamed.

"Pirates don't give you money," Big Mel shouted back. "They steal."

Aunt Phil said that was her point exactly.

Cali was standing back from the kitchen table as she always did when the family had a meeting. She tried to be like her mother—look at both sides. But these sides were too different. Her whole family was different. She was most like her mother, but she didn't have the patience. She wasn't anything like Phil—no one was—she and Lewis were from different planets. And Big Mel was sick of the store, sick of hardware, and just wanted to sell, get out, and move to Boise.

"Okay . . ." Her mom took out a legal pad and started

making a list. Making lists made Phil nuts because she never agreed with what got on the list. Big Mel didn't like lists someone else made.

"So how come you're so all-fired sure we've got to sell?" Phil shouted at Mel.

"Because I worked it out."

"Where?" Phil already knew the answer.

Big Mel pointed to his big head. "Here."

"And because of what's in your empty head, you want me to hand over the legacy of my father and his father before him, who had to flee from Cossacks to give us this home in a free land?"

Big Mel ate another doughnut. "They got on a boat from Ireland, Phil. There are no Cossacks in Ireland."

"Cossacks are everywhere," Phil growled and turned to Cali, who refused to make eye contact.

"Look," Mom offered, "I know emotions are running strong here—but we can't compete with a Waldo's across the street. No one can."

"The stench of their presence is filling my nostrils," Aunt Phil railed.

"People want a bargain, Phil. They want everything under one roof. It's how the world is. You can't fight it."

"My father built this store; his *soul* is between the floorboards."

Lewis, who had been spitting on the floor, stopped.

"He was ahead of his time, Phil," Mom said gently. "There weren't many hardware stores back then."

"He was a hardware prophet. He used to say to me, 'Phil,

I've given you a hard name for a girl because I want you to remember that life is hard. The hardware life is hard, but it's worth it because you make life better for people.'"

They went on like this for fifteen minutes.

Cali's mother took several aspirin.

Cali smoothed a split thumbnail with an emery board.

Lewis went back to spitting.

"We're going to have a vote," Cali's mother said, "in plain view of each other. All the partners and up-and-coming partners. We're going to raise our hands and show where we stand."

Cali didn't want to do this.

"How many think we should sell the store?"

Big Mel and Lewis shot their hands up.

Mom's went up sadly.

Phil grabbed her heart.

They all looked at Cali, who raised her hand a little. She didn't look at Phil when she did it.

"Okay, who thinks we should keep the store and fight?"

Phil's hand shot up.

Cali's hand went up a little.

"You can't vote twice!" Lewis shouted.

"I'm splitting my vote!" Cali shouted back.

Phil stood up, tears in her eyes, and motioned to Cali. "Hand me that hammer."

Cali did.

"A man can build a home with this tool. He can build a tree house for his child. He can build a boat that sails around the world."

"He can slam his thumb and need a Band-Aid." Lewis snickered.

"The words of a heartless person. If we sell the store, the day it changes hands, that's the day I'll drop dead."

Mom looked concerned. "Phil, you're not going to do something . . ."

"I'll die from a broken heart. You watch."

"Phil, we need to talk about this some more."

"Will it be on the steps? Who knows? Will it be on the street? Who knows? Will it be behind the counter?" She shrugged. "But I'll be dead. You'll have to step over my lifeless body."

Everyone sighed, looked down.

"Aunt Phil, the corpse," she added.

The vote held.

3.5 to 1.5.

They were selling the store.

"It could be any day now," Phil said, taking her temperature. "I feel my life slipping away."

Within two months, all the stores on Lattice Avenue had sold to Waldo.

Shut their doors, boxed up their memories.

"We didn't fight hard enough," Phil said. But no one was listening.

They packed up the bins of screws and crazy tools that nobody wanted. More nails than anyone could ever use. Cans of paint, brushes, rollers. All shoved in Phil's basement.

Phil refused to let it go.

Cali sat down there with her family's history packed in storage crates.

Her hardware legacy.

And she wasn't even handy.

Still, families are the strangest things. They can drive you nuts, make you run screaming into the night, but there is still *this connection.*

Cali wasn't sure what she was connecting to.

Maybe her memories of playing at the store when she was small, of hurling things at Lewis when he wasn't watching, of listening to people come in who had a problem in their homes they needed to fix.

Phil's Hardware had been there for eighty-three years to help, and now it was going to be turned into a parking lot. All the places she'd played as a child were going to be tarred and painted with white stripes.

She didn't know how to feel. She didn't want to run a hardware store when she was older.

She didn't want the store to not be in the family.

Even Lewis was conflicted.

He stood at the door in Aunt Phil's basement and said, "I had a dream last night about screwdrivers. All these screwdrivers were sitting at the dinner table, talking to me like they were family. One of them was my dad." Lewis's dad was Aunt Phil's second cousin. Lewis looked at Cali. "Do you think that's weird?"

"Yes," said Cali, and told him her dream about being stuck in a room with recessed lightbulbs that were all burned out.

"That's weirder," Lewis offered glumly while Waldo's

grand opening banner unfurled, proclaiming the big cosmic cop-out.

It was against the law to shoplift or snatch a purse, but it was legal for a huge conglomerate to knowingly build a store that will knock out all the little stores in the neighborhood.

It wasn't just legal.

It was good for the community.

Cossacks *are* everywhere. And they always have more money than you do.

Cali looked in her wallet. One dollar and sixty-seven cents.

That had to last her through the week.

Make do. That was what Mom said. She said that when Cali's dad walked out two years ago.

Make do.

Cali knew the routine.

Food and rent—that's where the money goes.

Eat macaroni and cheese over and over. Look for change under the sofa cushions.

No movies, except on TV. No eating out.

Making do is exhausting.

"I wish I could make it better for us," Mom said.

"It's okay, Mom. I'm okay."

Her mom seemed so sad these days.

Lewis did, too.

Cali could understand her mother's sadness—a single parent, a crazy family, deserted by her husband, looking for any work she could. Cali's mom had *cared* about the store, but *Lewis*.

He'd hardly worked a decent day at the store in his life. He'd put up a paper cup at the register: YOUR TIPS APPRECIATED.

Aunt Phil went ballistic when she saw that.

Lewis, undaunted, took the tip cup to school, put it on his desk, put it in front of him when he was eating lunch in the cafeteria. People would laugh and throw a dime, a nickel into the cup. He pulled in about a dollar fifty per week.

It made Cali crazy. "You've done nothing for that money!"

"That's not true. I've made people think."

Lewis didn't give a roaring rip about hardware.

So what was the big act now?

Waldo's opened in mid-April as the freshness of spring poked through the ground. Hundreds of red, white, and blue balloons and a brass band played in the parking lot. People flooded into the place as if Waldo's offered the secret to happiness at discount prices.

Cali didn't go to the grand opening.

No one did from Lattice Avenue, except Phil.

"I just want them to see my face," she announced. "See the whites of my eyes. See that I'm still standing."

Cali tried to work on her research paper for her favorite class at Roxbury High, business and marketing.

At least it had been her favorite class until this assignment.

"How would you pull a hurting business back together?" asked her teacher, Mr. Mack. "Think about it. Write your report."

Cali didn't have to think about it.

Oh sure, there were the typical textbook answers.

More advertising.

More public relations.

Cut costs.

But Cali knew from personal experience they didn't work.

How do you pull a hurting business back together when a Waldo SuperStore comes to town? Cali wrote this across her notes.

The answer is you don't.

So Cali wrote that up for her report.

Wrote up all the angst of the last two years.

How Waldo's approached the town of Sand River Junction, Iowa, and said after careful marketing and research, after seeing the down-home quality of this fine American town, *this* was where they wanted to build a new superstore that would really bring the folks in off the interstate.

"Think of the tourism," Waldo's community relations manager said.

The mayor and the town council thought of the tourism.

And Aunt Phil led the protest.

They got petitions signed.

They marched.

They got posters: WALDO, GO HOME.

But he didn't go.

He moved right in like a tornado touching down and taking everything in its path.

Cali had a photograph of a tornado in full funnel on the

cover of her report to make the point.

Mr. Mack said to her, "You didn't do the assignment."

"I thought I did. I couldn't think of it any way else except personally."

And she started to cry.

Stood there by the happy poster from the Small Business Administration proclaiming how small businesses make America work.

Stood there with fat tears running down her shirt.

The first person ever, probably, to cry in business and marketing.

But Mr. Mack was one of those teachers who cared more about the process of learning than if you got the question right.

"Cali, with your permission, I'd like the class to try to work at your problem."

"How does a little store fight against a giant?"

That's how Mr. Mack opened the class on Tuesday.

There were lots of answers.

Being better.

Being smarter.

Understanding what people really want and giving it to them.

Mr. Mack underlined that last one three times.

"Cali," he said, "what do people want from a hardware store?"

"Well . . . I guess they want fair prices; they want a lot of variety. They want someone who knows where everything is. They want people in the store they can ask questions because lots of people go in there and don't know what they're doing."

"Can a little store provide a more personal touch than a big one?" asked Mr. Mack.

Most students said yes, but Cali shook her head.

They didn't understand.

"Help us understand," Mr. Mack said to her.

And she didn't know how to tell them about her family and how they'd been linked to this store and helping people. How they'd all worked crazy hours, except for Lewis, and spent weekends and holidays together and it *all* centered around hardware. Christmas was about hardware. Easter, Fourth of July. There wasn't a holiday invented where the Business didn't come up. And Aunt Phil could build a house herself.

But none of that mattered now.

So she just said, "People don't want the personal touch anymore. They want bargains."

Mr. Mack took a step toward her. "I disagree," he said gently.

Fine, Cali thought. *It's your class.*

"Let's just say I'm right. How would a little hardware store overcome a big competitor like a Waldo's?"

Cali was getting angry.

She didn't want her family's problem up there on the blackboard.

"Any thoughts?" Mr. Mack asked.

"Find out what they do that is exceptional and unique," said Jason, "and stick to that."

"Don't forget," Cali shouted, "that money is tight and not

everyone in the family wants to keep the store going." She was embarrassed she'd said that.

Darla Green, who'd never looked for change behind the sofa in her life, gave Cali a pitying look.

Cali wanted to evaporate.

But Mr. Mack made it an assignment.

Due the end of the week.

Research the Waldo chain. Find their strengths and weaknesses.

Then build your business plan.

Don't skip steps.

And make it *good*.

Cali did the research, even though she didn't want to. This is what she found.

FACT: A Waldo's SuperStore opened up twice a week somewhere.

FACT: They paid their employees only minimum wage with second-rate health care benefits.

FACT: They did not have experts in their different departments.

FACT: Some products thrived in this discount environment. Others didn't.

FACT: Some shoppers left frustrated at the long lines and lack of information.

The next few days at school kids from business and marketing kept coming up to Cali.

Lloyd: "Say your family took your business on the Internet."

Darla: "Do you think you guys could start some kind of

business that gave advice to home owners who needed to do home repair projects?"

Jason: "What if you guys got a kiosk—you know, a booth—stuck it up across from the Waldo's. Kept most of your stock someplace else, and sold things right there on the street, gave advice on projects, that Waldo's could never do?"

Cali wasn't sure.

By the end of the week Jason said, "I think you face them down, but not in the old store. In a place they'd never expect you to be. In this booth with a big sign. And you could call the local papers and they'd give you free publicity, I bet. And I checked the zoning laws and all you have to do is get a license to have a cart or a kiosk. As long as you're thirty feet away from the front entrance of any store, it's legal."

"Jason, you're brilliant."

"I know. You want to go to a movie?"

"This is a great idea."

"Yeah, I've wanted us to go to a movie for a while now."

"No. The business plan."

But part of Jason's business plan was going to the movies.

"After we save your store, can we go to the movies?"

Cali ran out the door with Jason's business plan in her fist.

The rule in Cali's family was that anyone could call a family meeting and everyone had to come.

"I'll come if I'm not dead," said Aunt Phil.

They all sat there—Big Mel eating pizza, Lewis spitting, Mom nervous, Aunt Phil checking her pulse.

17

Cali laid out Jason's plan. Mentioned the Internet.

"It's too late," said Big Mel.

"I'm afraid he's right," said Mom. "We just have to move on."

"I think it could work," said Lewis.

Shock.

"I think it's worth a shot," Lewis added like the voice from the crypt.

Aunt Phil rose, raised her hands to the ceiling—a hardware prophet. "The sign could read: WE'VE GOT WHAT THEY DON'T HAVE."

Big Mel said that was stupid.

"No," shouted Lewis. "We kept the stock. We could have home delivery."

Aunt Phil grinned at Lewis. "I always knew you had the touch."

It took a month to get the license, for Lewis to paint the sign, for Jason to contact the newspapers and tell them what was happening. For Big Mel to move to Boise.

Aunt Phil was flushed with life as the kiosk got delivered, and she put up that covered booth thirty feet from Waldo's main entrance.

It was Cali's idea to have a one-month countdown.

ONLY THIRTY MORE DAYS TO GET WHAT THEY DON'T HAVE.

ONLY TWENTY-NINE MORE DAYS . . .

On and on.

The mystery built.

Excited people asked what was happening, and even Phil

kept her mouth shut, which Mom said was a sign, maybe, from God.

And on opening day, Phil had her balloons out just like Waldo's had had. She had a David and Goliath T-shirt made and gave them away to the first thirty customers.

That was Lewis's idea.

Jason passed out brochures to the crowd of people.

"Are you okay, Aunt Phil?" Cali asked when Phil was about to release the two pigeons (she couldn't afford doves) to signal that a new day had come to hardware.

"You remember this day," Phil told her. "You remember that we're all part of each other, comingled with these tools in this little cart. We will rise again or die trying."

Phil raised a premium hot-glue gun on sale for $29.95.

Cali nodded. She was so happy to see a Phil's Hardware sign back on Lattice Avenue.

A reporter elbowed her way through the crowd. "What are your thoughts on this day?" the reporter asked Phil as a photographer began taking pictures.

"It's just like how it was in the beginning with my father and his cart on the streets selling his tools from his father's blacksmith shop."

This wasn't exactly true, but it made a really good hardware story.

The general manager of Waldo's came out to shake Phil's hand and wish her well, but he was really letting everyone know he thought she was crazy.

"Watch this, big man," Phil said to the manager.

She released the pigeons.

The people oohed and ahed.

Those birds caught the wind and sent a stream of pigeon droppings on the giant Waldo head.

The photographer got a picture of that.

The people applauded.

No one was certain this would work, but it was sure worth a try.

And that very night, Cali and Jason went to the movies.

JOAN BAUER

is an award-winning novelist and short story writer. She received a Newbery Honor and Christopher Medal for her novel *Hope Was Here* and won the first *Los Angeles Times* Book Prize in the young adult fiction category for *Rules of the Road*, which also received the Golden Kite Award. A former journalist and screenwriter, she lives with her family in Brooklyn, New York.

Siskiyou Sloan
and the
Eye of the Giraffe
BY NORMA HOWE

Sisky had his hands full bathing the baby, so he wasn't able to answer the phone. He had the kid all bundled up in a towel now, slung under one arm, and he had just started to rummage through the dresser for some heavyweight sleepers, for it was November in Amherst, and there was no heater in the bedroom of their small apartment. It was Sisky's night for bedtime chores, and unlike Elly, who preferred to line everything up neatly beforehand, he reveled in the excitement and challenge of a one-handed search for a matching top and bottom before the hungry kid grew impatient and started to yell. Since the arrival of the baby, Sisky would be the first to admit that his criteria for excitement and challenge had spiraled down to a much lower plateau than he'd ever thought possible.

"It's your sister," Elly said, walking into the room, dusting a small cloud of white cake mix from her chest with one hand and tentatively holding out the phone with the other. "I think it's sort of bad news."

Sisky and Elly, with elbows all akimbo, awkwardly exchanged the phone and the baby for this was still a relatively unpracticed maneuver for them. "Ooh, ooh, ooh! Just a wet widdle guy, aren't you, lil' punky?" Elly bent her head toward the baby, her long brown mane falling all over his face, and gently tickled his towel-draped body with her nose. Then, bringing one hand up to her forehead, she parted her hair just far enough to watch how Sisky would take the news: Biscuit the dog was dead.

Sisky plugged one ear and held the phone as close as he could against the other.

"Hi," he said. "What's up?"

"I guess Elly didn't tell you, huh? Oh, God, Sisky. It's so awful! I hate to be the one to break the news, but Mom wouldn't do it and Yo's out somewhere, as usual—"

Sisky adjusted his silver-rimmed glasses by gently lifting them at the bridge, contorting his mouth like a goldfish about to suck in a tidbit of food. He glanced back at Elly, raising his brows and shaking his head, communicating his frustration at Toiyabe's typically indirect and cautious manner. "Come on, Toi," Sisky said. "Give it a try." Then he edged himself into the little nook of a kitchen and skillfully coaxed shut the flimsy sliding door without causing a major derailment, prepared to hear the worst.

"Well, it's Biscuit—"

Sisky brushed back a shock of Irish-black hair that had fallen over one eye and leaned against the stove for a second, but there was a cake baking in the oven and he could feel the heat, so he took a short step and leaned against the refrigerator instead. He knew at once, by the little tremor in her voice, that the old dog was dead.

"He was old, Toi," he said finally. "And you know he wasn't happy. God, when we were there in August, it took him half an hour just to stand up—"

"I know. But it's so sad. He—" His sister broke off.

Sisky took a deep breath and looked up at the stain-splotched ceiling above the stove, waiting for her to continue. When it became apparent that she wasn't going to speak without a bit of urging, Sisky stepped in to fill the void. "Come on, Toisy," he said, employing her favorite nickname for added inducement. "What is it? I'm listening."

"I *know* you're listening, but I can't tell you this part. I know what you'll say."

"I won't say anything. What is it?"

Sisky crossed his long legs and tapped his finger against the phone and waited.

"Well," said Toi finally, "when I found him this morning, he was lying on that Indian blanket you gave him that first Christmas after we got him. Remember? It was that Christmas after they got divorced. Just you and me and Mom and Yo. And Biscuit. And Mom saying—"

"I remember it, Toi," Sisky said. He didn't need her to remind him—their mother crying and saying this was our family now, and we all have to stick together, et cetera et cetera. "Go on. So you found him this morning, and what?"

"Well, he was lying on his Indian blanket with his little front paws touching each other, and honest to God, Sisky, it looked like he was praying—"

"Sheesh," Sisky breathed before he could stop himself.

"See there! I *knew* you'd say something like that!"

"I didn't say anything."

"You liar! I heard you! You said *sheesh*! Listen, Sisky, just because you're some kind of godless secular humanist, or whatever it is you call yourself, who doesn't believe in anything, that doesn't mean the whole world is like you!"

Just because you're some kind of godless secular humanist. It was their old argument, rising to the surface again—this time because of a dog. Sisky didn't know whether he would explode in anger, shouting her down until she finally realized that one person's faith is another person's lie—or simply bide his time and give this one to her, *because* of the dog.

Sisky swallowed. "Hey, calm down, okay?"

"Calm down yourself! And I don't care if you believe it or not, but I'm positive that Biscuit's in heaven right now! Here's Mom."

Sisky pulled up the chair with the little cushion that Elly made for him from a kit and sat down.

"Sisk?"

"Yeah. Hi, Mom."

"Everything all right? How's the baby? How's Elly?"

"We're all fine," he said.

"Well that's good." She paused a moment to clear her throat. "Uh, listen, I was wondering—I mean, I realize it's a lot of trouble for you, but do you think you kids could drive over on Saturday? You know, that baby of yours is three months old already and I've only seen him once."

Three months old! Wow! Could that be possible?

"I know it's a long ride," his mother went on, "but it's not like you live in California, for heaven's sake."

"Well, I—"

"The thing is," she continued, "we were planning to bury Biscuit in the yard tomorrow—you know, around in back of the garage where he loved to go digging all the time? But then

Toi got the idea to wait until Saturday, when we could have a more formal—well, not *formal*, exactly, but some kind of official family burial thing, you know, instead of just putting him in the ground and that's that. Yo said he could be here, if we had it after band practice. Hey!" she added brightly. "I already told you, didn't I, that only five kids were chosen to represent Kennedy High in this year's All-City Winter Band Concert and Yo was at the top of the list?"

Sisky wasn't fooled by his mother's lame attempt to forestall any questions about the so-called burial thing by distracting him with a reissued dispatch concerning Yo's musical achievements.

"Yeah, you already told me that. Good for Yo. But about Saturday, just what sort of official family burial thing is Toi thinking of? Will a member of the clergy be present? Will there be a choir? Will Yo play 'When the Saints Go Marching In' on his sax? Exactly how far does she plan to go with this?"

"Well, I don't know what —"

"Hey, Mom," he interrupted, "did she tell you about the pious position little Biscuit had assumed in his final hours? Wasn't *that* something?"

"Oh, Sisk. Cut it out." His mother lowered her voice. "Have a little *compassion*, can't you? You know how she is." Another pause. "Listen, hold on a sec, will you?"

Sisky opened the refrigerator door, looked around in there, and shut it again.

"Okay," his mother said. "She went to put some clothes in the dryer. She'll be back in a minute. Now, what were you saying?"

"You were the one doing the talking, Mom."

"Oh. Well, I was just going to say that you shouldn't underestimate how much she loved that dog, and I'm sorry I have to say this *again,* but you have no right to try to impose your beliefs—your *non*beliefs, actually—on her. If she wants to believe that dogs go to heaven, you should respect that. You know that Biscuit was like family, especially to her, and if she wants to pray for a member of her family—so to speak— well, that's her right and privilege."

Sisky cradled his forehead in his hand and let out an amazed little yelp. There was something about the way his mother always stood up for Toi that used to drive him mad with jealousy but which now appealed mostly to his admittedly warped sense of humor.

"Mom! Come on! Dogs in heaven? Even Father O'Malley didn't believe that. I heard him say so myself, one day in Sunday school."

"Well, times have changed. And if it's a comfort to her, it's none of your business, is it?"

Times have changed? Dogs are now allowed in heaven? Sisky smiled in spite of himself. Intellectually, he did understand the human need for comfort and assurance in an uncertain world—the drive, he felt, that prompts the majority of people on earth to embrace all manner of magical thinking— which, in his mind, encompasses everything from heaven and guardian angels to communicating with the dead and a belief in a personal God. But the fact that his own sister was included in this group was hard for him to comprehend; and he hoped one day he would find a way to point her to a more logical and scientific way of thinking.

"So what do you say?" his mother continued. "Do you want to drive over on Saturday?"

"No, I don't think so, Mom. The car's been acting up, and with the baby and everything, I just wouldn't want to risk it."

He hoped that would end the discussion. After all, there *was* some truth to it. Mr. Clunker had been in and out of the shop for months. And even though Sisky had great affection for the old dog, he was able to put his death in the proper perspective—aided greatly by the existence of his baby son, for the meaning of family now had a surprising and unexpected new dimension for him.

"How about the Greyhound, then? That's it! You kids could take the bus. Actually, when you think about it, it'd be easier than driving." His mother paused a moment and took a deep breath. "Well, if you want the truth, Sisk, we need you to dig the grave. I'm not up to it, and Toi couldn't possibly handle it emotionally, and Yo, well, he's always off someplace with Lowell . . ." Her voice drifted off.

Sisky sighed. There was the writing—right there on the wall.

"Mom, if *you* want the truth, here's the deal. I don't mind digging the hole, but I'm not sure I'm up to watching Toi do her praying thing out behind the garage." He wanted to work the phrase *captive audience* in there somewhere but realized he had missed his chance. So he settled for the I-might-crack routine. "I might crack, Mom. Really. I'm not kidding. You know how I am. I might set off an awful row. The whole idea is foolish and ridiculous and bizarre, and I can't be responsible for my actions."

"Sisk, honey, stop exaggerating. I'm sure you won't let that happen. I know you can control yourself. I've seen you do it. Now listen, let me pay for the bus tickets, okay? I realize money's a little tight—"

"Oh, jeez, Mom."

"So you'll come?"

Sisky thought he felt a strand of hair on his tongue, and now he was attempting to extract it with his thumb and forefinger.

"Sisk?"

Ah. There it was, spiraling along his fingers, with neither end in sight. He rubbed the tip of his tongue against his upper lip, just to be sure the specimen he had captured was the sole culprit. "Okay, Mom. You win. But I'll have to check with Elly."

"Well, I know she'll agree. Mothers always want to show off their babies. I know I did, with you three."

"Right."

"I'll make a roast or something. Did I tell you I managed to get the old crib down from the attic? It's all set up in the den, if you and Elly won't mind sleeping on the futon in there."

Sisky sighed. "No. We won't mind."

"I'm really sorry we had to call with such bad news—"

"Well, it's not exactly your fault that the dog died, is it, Mom?"

Sisky hated himself when he acted like that. But now he heard his sister's voice calling out loudly in the background. "Listen, brother dear! Biscuit *is* in heaven now! And I'd like to see you prove he isn't!"

Oh boy. There she goes again. "Hey, Mom, would you please

remind that nitwit sister of mine that the burden of proof lies with—"

"All right, that's enough!" His mother suddenly sounded very cross. "Nobody's proving anything! For heaven's sake! You two sound like you're still in elementary school, with your constant bickering and your prove its!"

Sisky cocked his head and wondered if he had heard her correctly. *Your constant bickering and your proovits.* Proovits? And then her meaning suddenly dawned on him, and he smiled.

"Sorry, Mom," he said. "So we'll see you on Saturday, right? We'll take an early bus. I'll check the schedule and let you know what time we'll arrive."

"That'll be fine," she answered, her voice almost back to normal. "I can't wait to see you all. And give my love to Elly and the baby."

"I will. 'Bye, Mom," he said, and hung up the phone, trying to remember when Toiyabe first started to taunt him with her *proovits.* It was probably during that disastrous family vacation at Disney World, back when they were kids. Oh, how she had bugged him on that trip! What a miserable five-year-old she was, pelting him with M&M's, messing up his stuff, spilling her milk shake on his Mickey Mouse ears, and worst of all, scribbling all over the pages of his books. And when he complained to his mother and father, Toi just stood there defiantly with her hands on her hips and repeated over and over with her annoying lisp a little phrase that she had actually picked up from him. "Puve it! Puve it!" she said, until he was ready to bop her one. His parents were no help at all. When they weren't arguing with each other, they were blaming *him* for everything.

"You're the oldest," his mom said. "Stop teasing your sister," his father instructed, both of them driving Sisky wild with anger and resentment. Ah, but finally, on the last day of their trip, he found a way to even the score. Even now, after all those years, he can still envision Toi's stuffed giraffe, her beloved Giraffy, balanced precariously where he had placed it on the railing around their third floor balcony, when, oops! What do you know? There it went, tumbling down and down, disappearing amid the branches of the magnolia tree below. And when her favorite little animal turned up missing at bedtime, oh, how the little brat did carry on, sniffling and crying the whole night through. But after they had returned home, her crying gradually gave way to prayer. *Please, God! Please bring back Giraffy! Please! Please!* In the meantime, she had stubbornly refused to be placated with other giraffes or substitute plush animals of any kind. Nothing, it turned out, but a real live dog could assuage her grief. Her mother finally found one at the shelter, a small mixed-breed terrier, already fully grown and housebroken. Toiyabe inexplicably named him Biscuit, and immediately took him to her heart, leaving Sisky to bathe in the comforting waters of his secret revenge for many years, calling upon that distant memory to tide him over whenever the forces of maternal favoritism and sibling injustice threatened to overtake him.

The next morning, because of the cake, Elly reluctantly suggested that they reverse their usual modes of transportation. She didn't trust Mr. Clunker and hated making the switch, but attempting to ride the Metro while carrying a birthday cake for her coworker was out of the question. So for today, she would take the car to work and drop off the baby at the sitter's, while Sisky took public transportation to school.

"Please, honey," she said now, reaching for her jacket. "Do me a favor and try not to bring home any more books from the thrift stores today. I know you're addicted, but we're so crowded now, there's hardly room for a fly."

"Well, we *could* get rid of the kid—"

Quick as a flash, Elly made a sudden underhanded grab for him, an unexpected move he hadn't known she'd possessed. It surprised him so much he reared backward and hit his elbow on the edge of the table.

"Ouch! That was my funny bone!"

"Serves you right," she said. Then, flipping back her hair, she adjusted the lid on the plastic cake dish and asked him if he would please carry their sleeping baby out to the car.

Sisky stopped in at the Salvation Army store first. Like a compulsive gambler, he was feeling lucky. Of the two thrift stores across from the Metro stop, the Salvation Army was usually the best. They had a whole room full of used books, and it was there that he had found the best one in his collection—an autographed copy of Mark Twain's *Letters from the Earth.* Well, not autographed by Mark Twain, unfortunately, but inscribed by Steve Allen, which really wasn't so bad: *For Roger Bingham, longtime friend and fellow agnostic, with all best wishes for CSICOP's continued success. Steve Allen.* Sisky loved showing that to people, because they would invariably ask about the meaning of CSICOP, and then he would have a chance to explain to them the purpose and mission of the Committee for the Scientific Investigation of Claims of the Paranormal.

It wasn't until after he had finished checking through the shelves of used books and was heading toward the door that Sisky accidentally spotted the stuffed giraffe on top of the heap in the toy animal bin. His breath caught in his throat, and for one of the few times in his life, he felt as if he had momentarily lost touch with reality, for there, nestled between a pink bunny rabbit and an orange lion with a ratty mane, was old Giraffy—Toiyabe's Giraffy—resurrected from the dead.

"Your family never ceases to amaze me," said Elly, fully embracing the cliché with a self-mocking smile.

The three of them were settled in the rear seat of the Greyhound now—Elly by the window, Sisky next to the john, and the baby, barely visible, ensconced between them like a little potentate in his secondhand car seat.

"Oh yeah? Like how?"

"Well, naming three kids after national forests, for starters."

"Actually, honey, Yosemite is a national park, not a forest."

"Whatever."

"Yes, but we mustn't sacrifice accuracy on the altar of hyperbole."

"Okay, so what about those annual arguments you guys have about canceling Christmas? You've been debating that since we were in high school."

Sisky shrugged. "Stay tuned. Toiyabe's the lone holdout, and one of these years I'll have her convinced."

"When chickens quack you will. But now, there's *this*."

"What's *this?*"

"Well, *this.* This little gathering of the family. Hey, I remember when your grandfather died, nobody hardly noticed. And now the dog keels over and you're holding a special memorial service."

Sisky smiled. She was good at exploiting the comedic opportunities presented by his family, but this time she purposefully overlooked the fact that his grandfather—a confirmed agnostic and author of a biography of Robert G. Ingersoll, America's Great Infidel—specifically requested no notice be taken of his death. Sisky was sure that he had inherited his own proclivity for unvarnished realism from his grandfather, just as Charles Darwin had discovered a foreshadowing of his great theory in the writings of his.

Sisky leaned over and kissed Elly briefly on the lips, and then reached across the seat for his old high school backpack—now stuffed with baby clothes and diapers. "Need this?" he asked.

"Not now."

He stood up and shoved it onto the rack above his head, giving it several two-handed pushes to make sure it would stay put. A smaller pack, embossed with the SUNY emblem, lay on the floor by his feet. It contained only a few books, in case he found time to work on his thesis, and the small stuffed giraffe from the Salvation Army.

A little while later, after Elly had fed the baby and both of them had dozed off, Sisky reached down, unzipped the backpack, and pulled out the giraffe. *My god! How long has it been? Fourteen years? Fifteen?* He reexamined the double-stitching on the leg seam and the worn spot along the side of its neck where Toiyabe used to rub it against her cheek. Yet, as much as it appeared to be old Giraffy himself, there was still something odd about it, something that was not quite right. Sisky tried to envision the last time he had seen it, propped on the balcony railing, its long neck flopping to the side, and then— oh! Sure! How could he have forgotten? One of Giraffy's eyes had been shattered in the dryer, yet the giraffe he was holding still had both of his intact.

Sisky sighed with relief. He was no longer obliged to believe the near impossible—that a stuffed animal last seen almost fifteen years ago falling from a balcony in Florida could suddenly appear in a thrift store in the suburbs of Buffalo. *Now, which eye should he remove?* While he couldn't be absolutely certain, his best recollection was that the left eye had to go. He reached into his pocket for his Swiss Army knife and flipped open the small pair of scissors. Then he pulled on the offending visual organ as hard as he could until he spotted a short length of thick white thread buried within. He snipped the thread and then returned the knife back to his pocket, along with the little yellow eye. There, he thought, holding the stuffed giraffe aloft. *That's more like it.*

Elly, suddenly awake, exclaimed in a loud whisper, "Yuk! Where'd *that* come from? It's filthy!"

"What, this?"

Elly glanced quickly at the still-sleeping baby and indulged in a cramped stretch, careful not to jiggle his car seat and risk awakening him. She reached for the giraffe and held it gingerly by its neck like a dirty sock. "God," she said, "this thing's a mess. Did you find it on the floor or what?" She motioned to the front of the bus. "Maybe one of those little kids up there dropped it on the way to the john." She examined it further, turning it backside up and fingering the faded label. "Made in China," she said. "All man-made materials."

Sisky turned and gazed at her, his high-school sweetheart, the mother of his child. He had never told anyone of his dastardly deed of long ago, but now he felt slightly giddy at the prospect of confessing at last.

"A long time ago, my sister used to have a giraffe like this, and I tossed it off the balcony of our hotel when we were at Disney World."

"You didn't! I don't believe it! What did she do? Did she run down and get it?"

"No. She didn't even know I did it. She still doesn't know. It landed in a tree. She never knew what happened to it."

"Jeez! What a rat!" Elly said, really more amused than alarmed at this unexpected glimpse into his childhood. "Oh-oh, look here. One of its eyes is missing."

"Yeah, I just pulled it out. Now it really looks like her old one. It had a missing eye, too."

"So what are you going to do with it? Are you going to surprise her with it?"

"Maybe," he said, avoiding her gaze. "I haven't decided yet. That's why we got the dog," he added, "you know, back then. Toi was so upset about losing the giraffe that my mom got her a dog."

"And now the dog dies and the giraffe returns. Boy, that's weird. Kind of gives me the chills, actually."

Sisky's expression went suddenly blank, as if all his energy and emotions were concentrated in his brain.

"Where'd you get it, anyway?"

"Pardon?"

"I said, where'd you find it?"

"Oh. Yesterday, at the Salvation Army. But that's not too strange, really. They probably made hundreds of them, even though this is the only one I've ever seen that's exactly like Toi's."

"Hmm." Elly nodded, then leaned her head back and closed her eyes.

After a few minutes Sisky mused aloud, "You know what I *could* do—"

Elly opened one eye and squinted at him.

"It'd be kind of a dirty trick, but I could use this giraffe here to—well, how to put this? Okay. Let's say I give it to her, like before we go bury the dog and everything, and I make up some story about how I hid it away that day it disappeared, and how now I'm really sorry about it, and feeling guilty and everything, with the dog dying and all, and I want her to have it back again."

"Yeah," Elly said cautiously. "Then what?"

"Well, then she's going to get all crazy and say how her prayers were answered and all that—"

"Will she say, *The Lord taketh away and the Lord giveth?*" asked Elly, all wide-eyed and innocent.

"Yeah. Maybe something like that."

"Oh, you nut."

"But wait. Then, a little later, I'll tell her the truth. I'll tell how I really found it in the thrift store, and it's actually *not* her same old Giraffy. And to prove it, I'll show her this eye, here—" Sisky reached into his pocket and pulled out the matching yellow eye. "And I'll make sure she gets the point— how her prayers *didn't* bring the real Giraffy back, and how this demonstrates on just a small scale how *easy* it is to believe only what you want to believe, even when there's no scientific basis for it at all."

"Well, I don't know about that," Elly said, picking up the little glass eye from the palm of his hand and examining it more closely. "I think you're way off base this time, Sisk, honey. I mean, why would you even want to do something like that?"

"Because that's the only way I can convince her of the pitfalls of that kind of thinking, that's why! Jesus, Elly—look around you! Look at all the trouble the world is in today! People are doing absolutely insane, violent, dreadful things every day, all in the name of religion! Look at the Middle East. Look at Northern Ireland, for God's sake! Christians, Muslims, Jews—all fighting each other, all believing that theirs, and *only* theirs, is the one true religion! It's crazy. It's insane. It's—"

"Sisky? Darling?" Elly said, reaching over and patting his knee. "Why do I have the feeling I've heard all of this before?"

"Oh? Have you? How could that be?" Sisky slumped back down in his seat. He took off his glasses and rubbed his eyes.

"I don't imagine your sister is about to commit any terrorist acts because she happens to believe in the power of prayer," Elly said dryly. "I think you're really going too far this time."

"Drastic times call for drastic measures," he said, putting his glasses back on and holding out his hand. "The eye, please."

41

"You're not really going to do that, are you? You're joking, right?" She held the eye between her thumb and index finger and raised it several inches before letting it drop into the palm of his hand.

Sisky returned the object to his pants pocket without comment and then carefully straightened out the rumpled little blanket covering the baby's legs. Pretty soon Elly settled back in her seat and stared out the window until she nodded off again.

Some time later a baby in the front of the bus started to cry, and Elly woke up with a start. She checked her watch. "It's almost noon," she said. "How much longer?"

"Twenty minutes, about." Sisky leaned over and looked down at the kid, who was still snoozing away. Then he took Elly's hand and gave it a little squeeze.

Toiyabe was waiting at the depot when they arrived, standing outside on the sidewalk where she had a good view of the buses as they pulled in.

"Oh, Sisk! Look at her!" Elly said, holding the baby across her shoulder and peering out the windows of the bus as they made their way to the front. "God, how forlorn!"

"Come on," Sisky said, bumping along the aisle behind her, carrying both the car seat and their bags. "Keep walking, please. We've still got a long day ahead."

"Here, Grandma," Elly said, gently placing the baby in her arms. "Does he resemble anyone you know?" she teased.

"Oh, I should say! Look at those eyes—so serious!" Sisky's mom carefully unwrapped the blanket from around the baby's legs. "And look how much he's grown! You probably don't notice it, Elly, since you see him every day, but I certainly can—"

"Oh, no," Elly said pleasantly. "I can see he's grown. He's even out of those little infant diapers already."

Across the room, Sisky and Toi exchanged glances, Sisky shrugging one shoulder, pretending he didn't know what all the fuss was about. "So, how's school?" he began. "Decided where you'll go after junior college?"

Toi shook her head. "I don't know," she said quietly, her eyes still red from the crying jag she'd had on the ride home from the depot. Sisky had offered to drive, and she readily took him up on it, climbing in the backseat next to Elly and the baby. "I'm really sorry about the dog," Elly had said, not referring to the animal by name, since she always thought that Biscuit was the most stupid name for a dog she'd ever heard, and she didn't want to risk revealing this prejudice either by her tone or facial expression. Still and all, proper name or no, Toi broke down.

"Well, how are your grades?" Sisky was asking now, as if he really cared. "Maybe you want to come to Amherst for your final two years," he suggested, then regretted it a moment later. He still had another year to go, and what if she said yes?

"Oh, no. Actually, I may drop out next quarter and get a job."

Well, it's now or never, Sisky thought. His backpack was still by the door where he had left it when they first came in. He went over now and picked it up and headed for the kitchen, unzipping it as he went. "Come in here a minute," he said, motioning with his head. "I've got something to show you."

"What is it? Do you want a drink?" she asked, following him to the kitchen and sitting down at the table.

"No thanks. Not now." Sisky cleared his throat. "Actually, I've got something to show you," he repeated, reaching into the backpack. "Remember when we went to Disney World that time?"

"Sure. What about it?"

He had the giraffe out of the backpack now, and was holding it under the table. "Do you remember this?" he asked, lifting it up in the air as if it were a winner's trophy.

"Giraffy!" she exclaimed, reaching out for it. "Oh, my lord! I've been praying about this for years! I've been praying that someday he'd come back to me!" She touched its eye and kissed it on the nose, and then she turned it over, stopping short when she spied the little label sewn to its underside. She stared at it for a long while, idly flipping it back and forth with her fingers, while the rush of excitement that had first enveloped her seemed to settle down into a kind of subdued acceptance. Finally, she smiled wanly at her brother and asked, "Where on earth did you find this?"

I knew it! I knew she'd think her prayers had been answered! "I don't know how to say this, exactly," Sisky said, suddenly appearing quite sheepish, "but I didn't *find* it anywhere. Actually, I—I've had it all this time. I've had it hidden away." Sisky swallowed, surprised at how naturally the words just flowed out of his mouth.

"But—" Toiyabe looked confused and puzzled. "But—"

"But what? I just hope you're not too mad at me. I was just a stupid kid, and you were such a pain in the—" He stopped short. "Well, you know. Anyway, I thought this would be a good time to—well, to make amends—because of, well, because of Biscuit and everything."

He watched her as she kept glancing back and forth from him to the giraffe, tracing her fingers across the yellow eye and then up around its ears and back again, as if she couldn't believe what he was saying. Sisky was so moved by the sight that he actually found himself blinking back a tear, and for a moment he almost believed his story was true, and he congratulated himself for keeping the giraffe safe for all those years.

"But, Sisk—" She hesitated.

"Yeah? What?"

But his sister just shook her head. "Nothing," she said.

"What? What is it?" Sisky persisted.

Then, still avoiding her brother's eyes, she placed the stuffed animal on the table in front of her and gently stroked its neck. "This is the nicest, sweetest thing you've ever done for me," she said at last. "I really mean it."

"You're not mad, then—"

She stared at him for a long time. "No," she said finally. "Of course I'm not mad. I was a little brat, and we both know it."

Sisky stood up. He knew she'd be touched, but he didn't expect that he would be, too. "Well, I guess I'd better—" He was going to say he guessed he'd better go out and start digging the grave, but instead he said, "I guess I'd better bring in the rest of the stuff from the car." He left her there, sitting at the kitchen table. Stage one of his plan had gone off without a hitch.

A few minutes later Toi heard the first little warning cries from the baby in the other room. She put down the scissors she was holding and tossed the little label in the garbage.

"Look, Mom!" she said, walking into the living room. "Look what Sisky brought me!"

"What is that? Is that Giraffy? Where on earth—" She took the giraffe into her lap and stared at it in amazement.

Elly, who had the baby propped up on her shoulder, jiggling him and patting his back, was also looking on with uncommon interest.

"He had it all the time! Can you believe it?" Toi said.

Her mother seemed almost as touched and amazed as Toi appeared to be. "Oh, honey!" she exclaimed. "Look! Remember when you cut off that label and nicked him with the scissors here in his behind?" She laughed and looked up at Elly. "Toi was so cute! She said Giraffy had *told* her he didn't like that label there on his butt, and he asked her to cut it off!"

"Oh?" said Elly, arching her eyebrows. "Really? That's pretty funny."

Sisky had the grave all dug by the time Yo arrived home from band practice with his friend Lowell in tow, the two of them, with identical streaks of pink in their hair, looking more like brothers than Yo and Sisky ever did.

Earlier, Toi had agonized about what to use for a coffin, finally deciding to wrap the dog in his Indian blanket and bury him in his toy box along with all his toys, even though that would leave only his leash and collar—plus the collection of yearly dog licenses—for her to remember him by.

The sky had grown overcast as the afternoon wore on, and now it looked like impending rain as the little group assembled around the newly dug grave in back of the garage, surrounded by a minefield of half-buried bones and chewed-up tennis balls.

Toi and her mother were standing side by side as Sisky lowered the toy box down into the hole, grimacing slightly as the rough earth scraped against the back of his hands, for he had forgotten to bring his gloves.

"Let's all hold hands now," suggested his mother in a quiet, subdued voice, "while Toiyabe joins us together in prayer."

Elly, standing between Toi and Yo, appeared mildly put off by the suggestion, but then gamely shifted the baby up a notch on her shoulder, supporting him from beneath with just one arm instead of two. Toi struggled to touch Elly's fingers, which were barely protruding from under the baby's blanket, while Yo clasped her free hand. Lowell, looking confused, took a step backward with a what-am-I-doing-here look on his ruddy face, but then Toi smiled at him weakly and said, "Please, Lowell, stay where you are. You're practically one of the family anyway."

Meanwhile, Sisky stood apart, leaning on the shovel, with his feet crossed at the ankles. "Sisky, come on," his mother urged. "Put down the shovel and join us over here."

"No, Mom," Toi said quickly. "It's okay."

Sisky, surprised, continued to lean on the shovel. He glanced up to see his sister acknowledge him with a nod and trembling lips. "If he doesn't want to, he doesn't have to."

Siskiyou Sloan stood tall and stayed his ground. While Toiyabe said a prayer in memory of her dog, he gazed upward toward heaven and saw only the bare limbs of the elm tree outlined against a cloudy sky. When the prayer was over, Toiyabe glanced at both Elly and Sisky in turn and said, "I just want to thank you guys for coming all this way. It's really nice that we could all be here together to say good-bye to Biscuit. You know, I've always been amazed at the ways in which prayers are answered," she continued, freeing her hand from her mother's comforting grip and slowly holding it up in front of her as if to quell the opposition, "but all I'm going to say about that is this: I may have lost one very special member of my family this week, but I surely gained another. God bless us all."

Although no one seemed to know exactly what she meant by that, her words were followed by a general murmur of assent, and, as if on cue, they all dropped hands and turned to leave. Sisky, however, remained behind to finish the task—returning the earth, shovelful by shovelful, pausing only long enough to drop into the hole a small glass object to mark the spot where tiny yellow flowers would someday bloom and grow.

NORMA HOWE

is the author of eight young adult novels, including the cele-brated Blue Avenger trilogy: *The Adventures of Blue Avenger* (a finalist for the California Young Reader Medal), *Blue Avenger Cracks the Code*, and *Blue Avenger and the Theory of Everything*. She lives with her husband in Sacramento, California.

Necessary Noise
BY EMMA DONOGHUE

May blew smoke out of the car window.

Her younger sister made an irritated sound between her teeth.

"I'm blowing it away from you," May told her.

"It comes right back in," said Martie. She leaned her elbows on the steering wheel and peered through the darkness between the streetlamps. "You told him to be at the corner of Fourth and Leroy at two, yeah?"

May inhaled, ignoring the question.

"Fifteen's way too young to go to clubs," observed Martie, tucking her hair behind one ear.

"I don't know," said May thoughtfully. "You're not even eighteen yet and you're totally middle-aged."

That was an old insult. Martie rolled her eyes. "Yeah, well, Laz is utterly immature. Dad shouldn't let him start clubbing yet, that's all I'm saying. I told Laz to let me talk to Dad, but he'd hung up already."

May flicked the remains of her cigarette into the gutter. Somewhere close by a siren yowled.

Martie was peering up at a dented sign. "It says *No Stopping*, but I can't tell if it applies when it's two A.M. Do you think we'll get towed?"

"Not as long as we're sitting in the car," said her elder sister, deadpan.

"If the traffic cops come by, I could always drive around the block."

May yawned.

"I guess Dad was feeling guilty about being away for Laz's birthday, so that's why he said he could go," said Martie glumly.

"Yeah, well the man's always feeling guilty about something."

Martie gave her sister a wary look. "It's not easy," she began. "It can't be easy for Dad, holding everything together."

"Does he?" asked May.

"Well, we all do. I mean, Dad may not do the cooking and laundry and stuff but he's still in charge. And it's hard when he's got to be on the road so much—"

"Oh, right, yeah, choking down all those Texas sirloins, I weep for him."

"He's not in Texas this week," said Martie. "He's in New Mexico."

May got out another cigarette, contemplated it, then shoved it back in the box.

"Are you still thinking of giving them up the day after your twenty-first?" asked Martie.

"Not if you remind me about it even one more time." May combed her long pale hair with both hands.

Silence fell, at least in the old Pontiac. Outside the streets droned and screamed in their nighttime way.

"Actually, I don't think Laz gives a shit that Dad's away for his birthday," remarked May at last. "I wouldn't have, when I was his age. Normal fifteen-year-olds don't want to celebrate with their parents or go on synchronized swimming courses or whatever it was you did for your fifteenth."

"Lifesaving," Martie told her coldly.

"Whatever. The guy wants to go to some under-eighteens hip-hop juice-bar thing where they won't even sell him a Bud, that doesn't seem like a problem to me, except that he better get his ass in gear," said May, tapping on the side of the car, "because I've got a party to go to."

"I told you you should have called a cab."

"I'm broke till payday. Besides, Dad only lets you use the car when he's away as long as you give me and Laz rides."

"You could use it yourself if you'd take some lessons," Martie pointed out.

"There's no point learning to drive in New York," said May witheringly. "Besides, next year I'll be off to Amsterdam and it's all bikes there."

"Motorbikes?"

"No, just bicycles."

Martie's eyebrows went up. "What are you going to do in Amsterdam, exactly?"

"I don't know. Hang out. It's just a fabulous city."

"You've never been," Martie pointed out.

"Yeah, but I've heard a lot about it."

Martie tapped a tune on the steering wheel. "It'll be weird if you go."

"Not if. When."

"When, then."

May yawned. "You're always complaining I never clean up round the apartment."

"Yeah, but when you're gone there'll still be Laz, and his mess will probably expand to fill the place."

"Oh, admit it," said May, "you love playing martyr mommy."

Martie gave her a bruised look. Then she scanned the street again, on both sides, as if her little brother might be lurking in the shadows. "This thing you're going to tonight," she said, "is it a dyke party?"

Her sister sighed. "It's just a party. With some dykes at it. I hope."

"Is Telisse going?"

"I don't know. She's not really doing the dyke thing anymore, anyway."

"Oh."

"Why?" her sister teased. "Did you like Telisse?"

"No, I just thought maybe you did," said Martie stiffly. She checked her watch in the yellow streetlamp. "Come on, Laz," she muttered. "I bet he's doing this deliberately. Testing our limits."

"God, you're so parental," May hooted. "No wonder Laz hates you."

"He does not."

"He does so! He's always telling you to get off his case. 'Get her off my fuckin' case, May!' he says to me." May's imitation of her brother's voice was gruff with testosterone.

"He doesn't mean he hates me," said Martie. "He doesn't actually hate any of us."

May groaned and shifted in her seat, leaned her head back, and shut her eyes. "G'night, Ma Walton. . . ."

The minutes lengthened. Martie peered into the rearview mirror. A truck went by slowly, picking up garbage bags. "We could call Laz on your cell phone," she said, "except he probably wouldn't hear it over the music. Maybe I should go in and look for him," she added under her breath. "Or no—I can't leave the car. Maybe you should go."

Her elder sister gave no sign of hearing that.

"There he is." Martie threw open the door in relief. "Laz!"

The boy was stumbling a little, head down.

"Come *on*," she cried. "We've been waiting. May's got a party to get to."

"What do you know—the boy is wasted," said May in amusement, turning her head as Laz struggled to fold his long legs into the backseat.

"He couldn't be," Martie told her. "It's a juice bar."

May giggled. "Now there's a first. *Teens Gain Access to Alcoholic Beverage.*"

"Okay, okay," said Martie, starting the car with a rumble. "Laz, are you in? Your seat belt." She waited.

"Can we just drive?" asked May.

" 'Anyone who doesn't wear a seat belt is a human missile,' " Martie quoted. "If I had to slam on the brakes suddenly, he could snap his neck."

"Oh Jesus, I'll snap yours in a minute if you don't get going. Laz!" snapped May, turning to face her brother. "Get your belt on now."

He grinned at her, his eyes drowned in his dark hair. His fingers fumbled with the catch of the seat belt.

The car moved off at last. "Good night, was it?" May asked over her shoulder at the next traffic light.

The only answer was the sound of retching.

"For god's sake, Laz!" wailed Martie, taking a sharp right. "Not on the seat covers!"

But the noises got worse.

"That's really vile," said May, breathing through her mouth as she rolled down her window as far as it would go.

"Are you all right now?" Martie asked her brother, peering in the mirror. "Do you want a Kleenex?" But he had slid down, out of sight. She wormed one hand into the back of the car, grabbed his knee. "Sit up, Laz."

"Leave him alone for a minute, why can't you?"

"May, he could choke on his own vomit!"

"You're being hysterical."

Martie twisted around again. "Laz! I said sit up now!"

"Okay, pull over," said May, for once sounding like the eldest.

"But—"

"You're going to cause a pileup. Stop the car."

Martie bit her lip and pulled over in front of a fire hydrant.

May got out and slammed her own door. She opened the one behind and bent in. "Laz?"

No answer.

She pulled him upright, wiped his mouth with his own sleeve. "He stinks." After a long minute, May said, in a different voice, "I think he may be on something."

"On something?"

"Laz? Wake up! Did you take something?"

"Like what? Like what?" repeated the younger sister, her hands gripping the steering wheel.

"Oh, god knows, Martie. I don't even know the names for what kids are taking these days. Laz!" May shouted, trying to lift his left eyelid.

The boy moaned something.

Martie let go of the wheel and started scrabbling in her sister's bag. "Where's your phone, May? I'm going to call 911."

May climbed over her brother's legs and wrenched the passenger door shut. "Are you kidding? Do you know how long they take to respond? We'll be faster driving to the emergency room."

"Which? Where?"

"I don't know, try Saint Jude's."

"You'll have to n-navigate for me," stammered Martie.

"I'm busy holding Laz's head out of this pool of vomit," said May, shrill. "Just go down Fourth—there'll be signs on Thirtieth. Move it!"

Martie drove faster than she ever had before. Laz didn't make a sound. May gripped him hard.

"You should be talking to him," Martie told her at a red light. "Keep him awake."

"I don't think he is awake."

"Is he asleep? He could be asleep."

"Oh, wake up, Martie!" snapped her elder sister. "He's out of it—he's unconscious."

"Is his windpipe open? Check his pulse."

"I can't tell." May was gripping her brother's limp wrist. "There's a pulse, but I think it's mine."

The light was still red. "Let me." Martie wrenched herself around, burst open her seat belt, squeezed one knee through the gap between the seats. "Laz?" she shouted, pressing her fingers against the side of her brother's damp throat.

"Shouldn't you—"

"Shut up. I'm listening."

Silence in the car, except for a little wheeze in Martie's breathing. She put her ear against her brother's mouth, as if she was asking for a kiss. Then the car behind sounded its horn, and Martie jerked back so fast she hit her head off the roof. "He's not—"

"What? What?"

More horns blared. "Green," roared May, blinking at the lights, and Martie slammed the car into drive.

"I think it fucked him up when Mom went off," said May. The sisters sat at the end of a row of orange seats in the emergency waiting area, their legs crossed in opposite directions. "They say the younger you are when something like that happens, the more it messes up your head."

"That's garbage," said Martie unsteadily, examining her cuticles. "Laz was too young; he wasn't even three. He doesn't remember Mom being at home, he doesn't know what she looked like apart from photos."

"He must remember her being missing," May pointed out. "You do."

"That's different. I was five." Elbows on her knees, Martie stared up at the wall, where a sign said UNNECESSARY NOISE PROHIBITED.

"That first couple of years, when all Dad fed us was out of cans—"

"She had postnatal depression that never got diagnosed," Martie put in. "That's what Dad says."

After a second, May shrugged.

"What does that mean?" Martie imitated the shrug.

"Well, yeah, that's what Dad *would* say," said May. "He'd got to say something. He couldn't just tell us, 'Hey kids, your mom took off for no reason.' " May pulled out her cigarettes. "I mean, we could all have something *undiagnosed*," she added scornfully.

Martie pointed at the NO SMOKING sign.

"I know. I know. I'm just seeing how many I've got left. What's taking them so long? You'd think at least they could tell us what's going on," barked May, looking at the reception desk.

Her younger sister watched her.

"At the hotel, did they say where Dad was?"

Martie shook her head. "Just that he wasn't back yet. They'll give him our message as soon as he comes in."

"He's probably boinking some Texan hooker."

"He's in New Mexico," said Martie furiously, "and you can just shut up. You don't know why Mom left any more than any of us. You were only eight." She added after a second, "I think it makes sense that she was depressed."

"Well, sure, it must have been pretty depressing pretending to be our mom if all the time she was longing to take off and never see us again."

"I hate it when you talk like that," said Martie through her teeth.

No answer.

"You think you're so *au fait* with the ways of the whole, like, world, when really you're just bitter and twisted."

May raised her eyes to heaven.

The woman behind the reception desk called out a name, and Martie jumped to her feet. Then she sat down again. "I thought she said Laurence. Laurence Coleman."

"No, it was something else."

"I forgot to get milk," said Martie irrelevantly. "Unless you did?"

May shook her head.

"Laz didn't get any dinner. I kept some couscous for him to microwave, but he didn't want it—he said it looked gross." Martie put her face in her hands.

"Take it easy," said her sister.

"They say if there's nothing lining the stomach . . ."

"He probably got some fries on the way to the club. I bet he had a burger and fries," said May.

Martie spoke through her fingers. "What could he have taken?"

"Nothing expensive," said May. "He's always broke."

"I just wish we knew, you know, why he did it."

"Oh, don't start the whole lecture on self-esteem and peer pressure," snapped May. "Look, everyone takes something sometime in their life."

"You say that because you did. Do," added Martie, her cheeks red. "It just better not have been you who gave it to him."

"For Christ's sake!" A woman with a child asleep on her stomach stared at them, and May brought her voice down. "I would never. I don't do anything scary, and if I did, I wouldn't give it to my moron brother."

"You can't know what's scary," said Martie miserably. "People can, like, die after half an Ecstasy tablet."

May let out a scornful puff of breath. "They said he was having fits in the cubicle. E doesn't give you fits."

Her sister sat hunched over. "You know when she asked us about our insurance provider?"

"Yeah. Thank God Dad's got family coverage in this job, at least."

"No, but I think she was calling them—the insurance people. She picked up the phone. Why would she call them right away?"

May shrugged.

Martie nibbled the edge of her thumb. "Do you think maybe they won't cover something . . . self-inflicted?"

"It's not like he jumped off the Brooklyn Bridge," said May coldly.

"But if he took it—"

"Shut up! We don't know what he took or what he thought it was. Get off his case!"

There was a long silence. "I care about Laz as much as you do," said Martie. "Probably more."

"Fine," said May, her voice tired.

Martie got up and walked off. She dawdled by the drinks machine and came back with something called Glucozip.

A girl had come into the waiting area, arm in arm with her mother. The girl had a deformed face, something red and terrible bulging between her huge lips. Martie looked away at once.

May whispered, "I didn't think that was possible."

"Don't stare," said Martie, mortified.

"She's put a pool ball in her mouth! I tried it once, but no way."

Martie looked over her shoulder. So that's what it was. "You tried to do that?" she repeated, turning on her elder sister. "Why would you do that?"

"I was thirteen or so—I don't know. It was a dare."

"That's not a reason!"

Her sister shrugged.

Martie sneaked another look at the girl with the ball in her mouth. The mother was scolding loudly. "Where's your so-called friends now, then?" The girl twisted her head, made a small moan in her throat.

Martie turned away again, and offered her sister some Glucozip. "You should, even if you don't feel thirsty," she urged. "We're probably dehydrated. Unless we're in shock, in which case they say you shouldn't drink anything, in case they have to operate."

May stared at her sister.

"Are your extremities cold?" Martie persisted.

"What do you know?" said May, harsh.

The younger sister looked away, took another drink. Her throat moved violently as she swallowed.

"One crappy first-aid-for-beginners course, and suddenly you're an expert?"

Martie took a breath, paused, then spoke after all. "I know more than you."

"Like what? Like what do you know?"

She spoke rapidly. "For instance, if someone's got no pulse and he's not breathing, he's dead. Technically."

"He fucking isn't!"

"Technically he is. That's the definition of death," Martie told her sister shakily. "It's not brain death but it's technically death, until they get the heart started again."

"It's you who's brain dead," growled May.

"I just—"

"I don't want to hear it!"

Silence. Martie, eyes shining, read the back of her can.

"They've probably infibrillated him," May told her coldly, "and now they're just letting him rest."

"I think you mean defibrillate."

"I don't think so," snapped May. "And also, they've got chemicals they can use. There was that scene in *Pulp Fiction*, when Uma Thurman snorts heroin by mistake, and they stick an adrenaline needle in her heart."

"I can't stand that kind of film," said Martie. "They're totally unreal."

"No, they're too real," her sister told her, "that's what you can't stand." She let out a long breath. "When are they going to tell us something?" she said, leaping to her feet. "I mean, Jesus!"

"Could you keep your voice down?" whispered Martie. "Everybody's staring."

"So?" roared May. "I mean, what the fuck does that mean?" She threw out her arm at the sign that said UNNECESSARY NOISE PROHIBITED. "What the hell is unnecessary noise? If I make a noise, it's because I need to."

"You don't need to shout."

"Yes I do!"

Martie seized her elder sister by the hand and pulled her back into her seat. May went limp. Her head hung down. The people who had been watching looked away again.

"Do you think," Martie asked May half an hour later, "I

know this probably sounds really stupid, but do you think it's any use? Do you think it's any help to people, if you're, you know, there?"

"Where?" asked May, eyes vacant, taking a sip of Glucozip.

"Near them. Thinking about them."

"Like, faith healing?"

Martie's mouth twisted. "Not necessarily. I just mean, is it doing Laz any good that we're here?"

"I don't know," said May. "I think maybe we're irrelevant," she added slowly, without bitterness. "He never liked either of us that much in the first place."

"You don't have to like your family," said Martie uncertainly.

"Just as well," said May under her breath. "Just as well."

"Laurence Coleman? Laurence Coleman?"

They both registered the words at last, and jerked in their seats. "He's not here," said Martie to the man in the white coat, whose small badge said DR. P. J. HASSID. "They took him in there," she said, pointing vaguely.

"If you would come this way—"

They both scurried after Dr. Hassid. May plucked at the doctor's sleeve. "Is he alive?" she asked, and burst into tears.

Martie stared at her elder sister. Tears were dripping from her chin. One of them landed on the scuffed floor of the corridor.

"Just about, yes," said Dr. Hassid, not stopping. There were dark bags under his eyes.

Laz, lying in a cubicle, didn't look alive. He was stretched out on his back like a specimen of an alien, with tubes up his nose, machines barricading. May wailed aloud. Martie took hold of her elbow.

"No problem," said Dr. Hassid, fiddling with a valve. "There's no problem. Have a cry. How old is Laurence?" he asked Martie.

"Fifteen."

"Laz," May sobbed the word. "He's called Laz."

"It doesn't matter," said Martie.

But Dr. Hassid was amending the clipboard that hung at the end of the bed. "*L-A-S?*"

"*Z.*" May gulped.

"*L-A-Z*, very good. It's better to use the familiar name. Laz?" the doctor said, louder, bending over the boy. "Will you wake up now?"

One eyelid quivered. Then both. The boy blinked at his sisters.

EMMA DONOGHUE

is an Irish writer, playwright, and historian who now lives in Canada. Her novels include *Stir-Fry, Hood, Kissing the Witch* (a sequence of young adult fairy tales), *Slammerkin,* and *The Woman Who Gave Birth to Rabbits.* Her work has been translated into German, Dutch, and Swedish.

The Throwaway:
A Suite

BY NIKKI GRIMES

HOMELESS

This morning
my mother's words
fell like a knife,
splitting my life into
Before and After.
She pushed her way
into my tent
at first light,
breathing fear
or fire—
I'm not sure which.
"Wake up, Ishmael!"
she ordered.
"Pack your things.
We're leaving."
What?
I rubbed my eyes,
but there was
no nightmare
to wake up from.
"Hurry," she said
as if I could,
or would
rush to leave
home.

STRAIGHT TALK

Help me out here, Lord.
Just last week
I fell asleep
on the pillow
of my father's
familiar prayer:
"Lord, Jehovah,
bless my sons."
For years,
I was the only one
to speak of.
Don't tell me his love
was a trick
of my imagination.
So why this insanity?
Sending my mother and me
into the wilderness?
What did I miss, God?
What did I do
to chase away
his love?

BABY BROTHER

I'll miss bouncing Isaac
on my knee,
lost in his laughter,
wrapped 'round the finger
of the little brother
who makes me second best.
But I can do without
those other times
when I remember
he is the Promised One,
and I shove him aside,
my jealousy a stutter
I can't control.
"L-leave me alone!"
I snap, happy when he
toddles off whole,
spared from
the jagged edge of
my twisted love.

THE THROWAWAY

I burn here in the dust,
my tongue swollen as a fig,
chapped lips curled into
an awful grin.
My name is the joke
I laugh at:
"God heard."
Did he really?
Did he ever?
Look at you, Mother,
trembling
a bowshot away,
your tears
the only water
for miles.
At least you could
have stayed close
to share them with me.
But then,
why should you be
any different?
Everyone else
has left me alone.
My own father
has thrown me away.
So tell me, God.
Are you happy now?

THEN

Then came the water
split from rock,
proof that you're
as good as your word.
Angry or not,
I drink, hoping
you'll enlighten me:
Why this miracle?
Why not change
the heart of Sarah,
bless me with the family
of my dreams?
But then again,
you're no fiction.
Any god I fashioned
would sure as hell
give me what I want.
Instead,
you offer me
the mystery
of You.

FAST FORWARD

And what was there for me
all the years between
then and now
except the memory
of your promise
       to make me great
       to give me princes
       to stand at my shoulder.
Ever the ultimate insider,
I suppose this was your way
of letting me know
survival was never
in question.
Even so, a promise
is cold comfort
for a lonely son
spitting curses by the fire.
Yet, you were there
as promised,
whispering sweet nothings
in my mother's ear,
coaxing me to flex my bow,
checking the progress
of each arrow,
looking out for me
as only a parent would,
being the one father
I could count on.

NIKKI GRIMES

is a poet, novelist, journalist, lecturer, and educator. Her books *Meet Danitra Brown* and *Jazmin's Notebook* were selected as Coretta Scott King Honor books, while *Jazmin's Notebook* and *My Man Blue* were also selected as ALA *Booklist* Editors' Choices. She lives in Southern California.

Visit

BY WALTER DEAN MYERS

"**Y**ou have thirty minutes," the guard says. He nods toward a gray table with straight-backed chairs on either side.

I start to sit as the other door, the one not for visitors, opens. I try to smile as he walks toward me. *Oh, God, he is so young.*

"Hey, what's happening?" A smile flickers across the broad, brown face. There are pimples on his forehead.

We shake hands. It is the first time we have touched for twenty years. He sits. I sit.

"Have you heard anything?" I ask.

"Nah. How you doing?" His eyes dart away.

"I'm okay."

"I guess you're surprised to hear from me?"

The smile again flickers across the face. His eyes are downcast.

"A little," I say.

"I didn't have nobody else to put on the list."

"Hey, it's all good," I hear myself saying. "So, how are you doing?"

"I'm watching the clock, and the clock is watching me," he says.

"I know what you mean," I lie. I don't know what he means, not inside, not the way he feels.

"They wouldn't let me bring anything."

"I don't need anything," he says. "I was thinking . . ." His voice trails off, he looks away, toward nothing, toward the gray cinder-block wall. There are heavy seconds of silence.

"It's been a long time," I say.

"I didn't remember how you looked," he says.

His eyes search my face. He is searching for recognition.

"It was at Johnnie Mae's house," I say. "She had a cold and you had a cold. I went down to the drugstore for some cold medicine."

"How old was I?" he asks.

"Three? Maybe three, or two," I answer.

"More than twenty years ago."

"A long time."

"Well, what happened was that things went all right for a while," he says. He shifts his body. "Then they got confused."

I nod. He has a story to tell. I'll listen.

Another moment of silence. On the wall, the round prison clock looks down like the true face of God.

"Where were you living?" I ask.

"On 141st Street," he says. "You know where the building fell down?"

"Yes," I lie.

"We were living down the street from there," he said. "Near the playground. And she was on the pipe."

Johnnie Mae. I hadn't seen her in years. Dark. Wide-eyed. Wide-hipped. Black tree-trunk thighs that moved like thunder in the night.

"What did you do?"

"Hung out, mostly," he says. "I wasn't doing right, you know."

Confession.

"Sometimes it's hard to do the right thing," I say.

"No, man, you can do the right thing if you want to."

He glances up at the clock. It's four o'clock.

"So . . ." he continues. "I got in with this bunch of dudes. Flaky dudes, really. We did a little of this and a little of that. Sold some weed, did some jacking. Some jive get-overs. Nothing real—you know what I mean?"

"Yeah."

"Then one day this dude calls me up and wants to know if I wanted to get paid for nothing." He is talking faster. "I asked him what he meant and he said he had a walk through and all he needed was a lookout. I knew you didn't get paid for nothing, but I went along with the program. I was wrong right there."

Bless me, father, for I have sinned.

"Sometimes," I say, "you can't tell. . . ."

"So, what did you think when you heard about it?"

"I was disappointed," I lie. I didn't hear about it. I read about the appeal that was turned down in the newspaper on the A train going up to Harlem. There was no connection between us, no father-and-son thing that would have sent the calls from mothers, grandmothers, brothers buzzing through the city streets. "I was hoping it wasn't true."

We watch the clock, the clock watches us.

"It was supposed to be a push in," he continues. "He said this old woman had a heavy stash up in her mattress. He was going to push in and take the money, and we were going just to hang out like nothing happened because she never came out of the house and wouldn't know who we were if she saw us."

"Just the two of you?"

"Yeah. He was going to do the thing and I was just supposed to sit out on the steps and keep an eye out for people
coming off the elevator. But he took a few hits—I think he
was using crack or something—to get his thing together
before he went in. Then he went in while I was out sitting on
the stairs. Then he come out and said that the thing was going
down wrong. He needed me in there."

"You went in?"

"Yeah. I should have split right then and there, but I went
in," he says. "The old woman was laying on the floor, all angled
up and moaning. And there was her husband, he's sitting in a
wheelchair, shaking and carrying on and crying about his wife."

"Oh, God."

"I know you hate to hear that," he says. "You didn't think
I was going to ever get into nothing like that, right?"

"I was hoping . . ."

"Randy—that's the guy I'm backing up—he didn't know
anything about her husband even being there. And we're sitting there wondering what to do."

"Why didn't you just walk away?"

"Because the woman looks like she's dead," he says.
"According to the medical examiner, she was, like, mortally
wounded."

The missing years take invisible shape and sit between us.
I keep my eyes away from the clock.

"And?" I ask.

"Then Randy says we got to off the old man. There's a

hammer in the kitchen. You know, if he had shot him and there wasn't so much . . ."

Pause. My stomach turns. *Flesh of my flesh. Blood of my blood.*

"So much blood?" I had read the newspaper accounts.

"Yeah. Maybe it would have been different," he says. "It would have been the same, but not so, like, brutal."

"Yeah."

"You know, I'm sorry about this whole thing," he says. "They said I didn't have no remorse but, really, I was in such a deep shock kind of thing, I didn't even know what I was saying or doing."

"It was seven years ago," I said. "You were only seventeen."

"Eighteen," he corrects me.

"Eighteen."

"I'm sorry, too," I say. The hulking silence leans forward, peering into our faces.

"So." He leans away. "How did you and Moms meet?"

How did his mother and I meet? How to get a thousand years into the minutes we have left?

"I was looking for a place to live. I found a kitchenette on 115th Street. Most of the people in the place were on welfare. I was a step up, maybe a half step up, because I had a job. I was working in the garment center, down on 32nd Street. I had taken the test for the post office and was notified right after I moved into that place that I had passed."

"She was living there?"

His continuance is history. I am his father, and, as the bearer of his future, as the teller of his story, I am also his son.

"Yes. She had your brother, Tyrell. He was four at the

time," I say. "Then we met and started going together."

"Y'all were in looooove?" he says, drawing the word out. Desperately trying to lighten the moment.

Black tree-trunk thighs that moved like thunder in the night.

"We were in love," I say.

He glances toward the clock.

"I thought it was something like that," he says. "Y'all were both young."

"I can't believe how young we were," I say.

"Anyway, Randy was tripping ..." he continues, needing to go on with his story.

"You were in the apartment ..."

"And I'm like shocked because I never saw so much blood—no, it's like I never seen people hurt like that. One minute they're like people and then they're like whimpering and crying and they're something else."

"That had to be hard."

"That's not me, man," he says. "Hurting people like that. That's not me."

He looks away. There are tears streaming down his face, down the cheekbones that mimic mine, diagonally down along the light brown jawline that is mine, that is the jawline of the grandfather he has never seen.

"I know it's not you," I say.

"So Randy and I split and I don't want anything to do with him because the whole thing is foul and I know we've blown the set big time," he says. "You know what I mean?"

"Yeah."

"But it's done, man," he says. "Ain't no rerun, ain't no

thinking about how it should have ended."

"It's done," I echo.

"And it's me."

The voice is so quiet, so childlike. We are in the giddy vortex of what might have been, trying to catch the long-past moments.

"And it's you, son."

"I'm thinking about a new beginning, about starting my whole life all over again, and at the same time I know that this whole thing is going to end everything," he says. "Now I got this weight on me and I can't get out from under it."

Precious seconds pass before my mouth can open.

"I don't have all the answers," I say. "But sometimes I think that what we all have to do is to make peace within ourselves. To find our own connection with God and deal with that."

"When I got real scared," he says. "I was over at the market on 125th Street, you know where the train goes over and they sell candles and stuff underneath?"

"Yes."

"I was over there one morning," he says. "Real early. I couldn't sleep because I was so nervous after the story hit the papers. But I was thinking what you would feel if you saw my picture in the paper and everything."

"I was hurt," I lie.

Is the lie the better thing? Should I say I didn't know they were talking about a child of mine?

"I knew you would be, man," he says. He is asking for my pain to match his own. He starts to move his hand across the table, then stops and glances toward the guard in the corner of the room. We are not allowed to touch. "I knew you would be."

He turns his face away, and I know he is crying again. He is crying for himself, for this moment, and for all the moments that will never be.

The last time I saw him he was sullen, and he smelled of the cocoa butter his mother had smeared on his face to keep it from looking ashy. Her apartment was dirty; there were clothes piled in a corner. A straightening iron lay on the sink next to a bottle of cough medicine. They all had colds. Later, when it was time to leave, as I walked through the damp hallways I held my breath against the stench and made promises, to myself, of Christmas gifts that I would never fulfill.

Bless me, father, for I have sinned.

"And then what happened?" I ask.

"Then I got picked up and life just fell apart. The trial, lawyers, appeals, the whole nine yards," he says. "And here I am facing this heavy thing and I don't hear from nobody. But I know what's going down with you because she told me."

"She told you?"

"She told me that you and her met up and almost got married," he says. "She said her aunt didn't want her to marry you because you was too young or something."

I was nineteen and she was twenty-two, maybe twenty-three. She had long before acquired the habit of being used and I had the lust to use her.

"We were both young," I say.

"So, what you been doing, man?"

"Not that much, really," I say.

Now it is time for my confession, but I can't bring myself to it. I struggle to just get through the minutes.

"You got hands like mine, long, skinny fingers like mine," he says.

"Yeah, your mom liked my hands," I say. "But we drifted apart, then we lost touch."

"She said she saw you in Brooklyn," he says.

"I was buying pastry at Junior's Restaurant," I said. "We met and had a few words. She was looking great."

She was looking terrible. Her skin, which had always been so smooth, had looked dull and dry. Her eyes, the bright, incredibly innocent eyes that had made me smile a thousand times, were distant and desperate.

I walked away from her, away from you.

"I've been doing well," I say.

"I'm glad to hear that," he says. "You know what I was thinking? I know it's impossible, but you know what I was thinking?"

"What?"

"I heard they write down your last day," he says. "What you do and what you eat and stuff."

I glance at the clock.

"The clock is a bitch, huh?" he says.

"Yes, it is."

"What I been thinking about is, like when they write down the record and everything, they can write about you and me sitting here talking," he says. "Then when it's time to go, it's time to go. But, like, on the record, it's just me talking to my father. Like it's no big deal."

Bless me father, for I have sinned.

"No big deal?" I push the words out.

"Somebody comes across the record—about what happened—and it's a regular . . . thing." A thin finger flicks away a drop of sweat on the still-unlined forehead. "You dig it?"

"I think I do."

"I'm real glad we got to sit down like this because it means a lot to me," he says. "Because I don't think I'm all that bad a person and I think you can get next to that. I'm just like an ordinary son. You know what I mean?"

"I don't know," I say. "I think I could have done better for you."

Precious seconds go by, and I think we both want to end them.

"No, you're okay," he says quickly. *He wants me to be okay.* "We both have to figure out some kind of thing to do. I got to go where I got to go, and you got to be moving on. But we're here talking and everybody's checking us out and putting it all down for the record so I guess it's cool."

So little. There will be a record of a father and a son sitting and talking, having one last conversation, a babble of confessions tossed upon the fire.

"So I want to say . . . forgive me," I hear the words coming from my mouth. "So I want to say . . . forgive me and know that I know I haven't . . . haven't what?"

"Haven't done your best?" he says.

"Haven't done my best," I answer.

"We're embarrassed, right?" he says.

"I think so."

"You know, that's how I thought you would be," he says.

"I thought we would be sitting here thinking the same things and feeling the same way."

"Damn, this is hard."

"Yo, don't cry, man," he says. He touches my hand and the guard allows it. "It's not your fault. I threw it away. I just threw it all away. Sometimes it happens that way."

He pats my hand. He is comforting me. He smiles and stands before the guard gets to us. I had wondered if there would be a glass partition between us, or bars. There weren't. The last seconds in the visiting room are filled with his looking into my face and smiling. Him patting my hand in reassurance. Him saying good-bye.

There is one more scene. I sit with strangers, all of us uneasy in the grim theater of our fears. The curtains are closed. There is a nervous buzz of conversation in the room. I am tight with anticipation. In the corner of the room there is a nun, whiter than she is supposed to be, her habit darker than it should be. A million thoughts fly through my mind like demented harpies through the hot winds of hell. I look for the lofty thought, the God saving thought.

The curtains open. I know he will search for me. I know he has searched for me all of these years.

In the darkened theater there is a hush, a stillness that kills us all. His eyes find mine. They close.

WALTER DEAN MYERS

is a five-time winner of the Coretta Scott King Award and a recipient of the Margaret A. Edwards Award for Lifetime Achievement in Young Adult Literature. His novel *Monster* was winner of the first Michael L. Printz Award and was also a National Book Award finalist, a Coretta Scott King Honor Book, and a *Boston Globe–Horn Book* Honor Book. He lives with his family in Jersey City, New Jersey.

A Family Illness:
A Mom-Son
Conversation

JOYCE CAROL THOMAS

I. PROLOGUE

Mom

I had been calling your father, my first cousin Roz, bosom buddies, everybody. But nobody would believe that something was wrong.

You looked different, Champ. Not your quick, funny seventeen-year-old self. You moved in a disconnected way. You held down sidewalks with your best friends, Ace, Ryan, Stevie, and a slew of foulmouthed hoodlums. When darkness came and your curfew passed, I drove up and down the streets looking for you. On the liquor store corner, you wobbled back and forth, holding a king-sized bottle of rotgut.

Champ! You better get your Colt 45 butt in this car!

Where was my grace?!

In the laundry as I shook out your Shrink-to-Fit Levi's 501s, funny pills dropped on the linoleum.

Now what are these?

You didn't answer.

Son

You said I was mad the day I lifted the big, solid-wood swinging door between the dining room and the kitchen completely off its hinges. So splintered it couldn't be fixed.

When you said, "Stop it!" I cursed you out.

You told me years later that at that moment, you knew something was wrong and it wasn't just my hormones.

II. CONVERSATION
Son

Loud demands rumbling in my ear. Jumping demons cussing me out through the switch on the bedside lamp. I drank Old English malt liquor so strong my gangsta friends poured it in their gas tanks to start up their cars. But it didn't drown out the voices. I hurt. I hid in sleep, in alcohol, in pills. And I was scared.

Mom

Finally help was on the way. Cousin Roz, who was a mental health "professional," and her psychotherapist sidekick strolled up the walk. I opened the door before they could knock. The two sat on the couch side by side.

"Wake him up," bellowed the psychotherapist.

You trailed me downstairs still dressed in your pajamas. It was three o'clock in the afternoon. The therapist asked you a few questions. You answered, and then slumped back up to bed.

"There's nothing wrong with that insolent young man," the therapist said as he elbowed our cousin Roz. "He's just lazy."

"Lazy? No," I said. "I know lazy and this is different."

Cousin Roz woo-hooed, her way-in-the-back-of-her-mouth tonsils gargling laughter.

The therapist scratched his hairy chin and then spoke. Static in his voice: "We work with really crazy people all the time at the mental health clinic in Contra Costa County," he said. "And your son's slow as a slug."

"A biblical sloth!" he said, pink eyes, streaked with tired strings, bulged. Bubble gum ready to pop.

"Woo-hoo! Biblical sloth!" Cousin Roz giggled the words, tasting each spicy syllable. "Here's what we do to crazy folks," she added. She licked her lips. Fluttered her eyelashes. "This teenager dressed in dirty rags and loaded down with backpacks had a ring of smudge around her neck black as a coon's. Woo!"

"How old was she?" I asked.

"Sixteen. Snaggle-toothed. Guess she thought she was a woman. Titties out to here. No panties. Smelled her before she hit the door of the treatment room. Talking about nasty!

"We fixed her though. Took her to the bathroom. Dumped pots of boiling water in the tub 'til it was full, poured bleach in, and threw her butt in. She screamed so loud you could hear her all the way from Sacramento to Tijuana!

"Woo-hooey!" Cousin Roz wiggled her head, her arms, her legs, her feet mocking the tortured teenager.

So that's what they do to crazy folks.

I could never do that to you.

The minute they left I made an emergency appointment for you at Kaiser for ten A.M. the next morning.

Son

Mom, it was hard not to like Cousin Roz. She was funny. Her whole body shook like a boom box when she laughed. She made everything, even sad things, funny. If you broke your leg, she'd make a joke out of it, cracking up as tears slid down her face. I needed her. I needed everybody in my family. They all have a good side. But they hurt.

Son

The voices got so bad I shouted at the lamp switch, "Shut the ugly up!"

Then a tiger slithered from the lamp base to the floor and bellowed, "Kill yourself."

I didn't go out. Not even to the store. I didn't talk to anyone. It hurt when somebody touched me. Downstairs the phone rang, deafening and shrill as the security alarm.

A mosquito whined so loud the noise broke the sound barrier.

When the shadow on the front porch curled into a bundle of scorpions and rattlesnakes, people just walked on through them without blinking an eyelash.

"Why are you talking to yourself?" you asked.

"To myself? You don't pay attention. Didn't you hear them? Don't you know I was answering loud stuttering voices?"

Mom

The doctor at Kaiser Hospital asked you a question. "Have you ever tried to commit suicide?"

"Yes," you answered.

"When?" he asked.

"Today."

"How?"

"I took a whole bottle of aspirins."

Suicide?

I panicked. A little later and I'd have lost you.

They wheeled you into the emergency room and pumped your stomach out.

The doctor said as he scribbled in your chart, "I've made an appointment for you to check him into the clinic in Martinez for three days. They'll get him started on medication. It may take even longer."

Driving you to the out-of-town clinic, I was so scared.

Nobody I asked would go with me. Your dad didn't believe there was anything wrong, so he wouldn't come.

At the clinic, you shook with wild-eyed rage when they said you had to stay. I tried to calm you, but you were too strong. I couldn't hold you, hug you.

When the attendants grabbed you, you gave me a look that I'll never forget.

A look that said I had betrayed you. I remembered what they did to crazy people.

Attendants sedated you, strapped you down.

That look, that look you shot me, cut through me like a knife.

Son

Mom, you lied.

First you fooled me into going to that place. You didn't tell me ahead of time. You acted like we were going to a backyard barbeque.

You lied. You said it would be three days.

I stayed in the clinic bed. Too tired to lift my head from the pillow.

Too exhausted to participate in daisy chain, papier-mâché activities. Except I did an etching of Kool-blue monsters in the rec room.

You came to visit every day. You kept vigil, making sure the clinic staff knew you were present and that I was not alone.

As if that made a difference in how they treated me!

They told you not to check in so often. And like a nut case you listened. I couldn't believe it. Couldn't believe you!

You liked the monster etching so much I let you take it with you.

I still didn't trust you. You said three days. Then the staff had a meeting and said I had to stay longer. I wanted to leave. I wanted to go home to my own bed.

"You can't," you said on your next visit.

"You're letting them poison me," I yelled.

Right off the voices in my mind shouted, right on.

And you left me in that hellhole with nobody to stand between me and a tub of boiling water.

Mom

Champ, I wonder. Was it the divorce?

I was fuming when his attorney, in order to give him the advantage, told those outrageous lies on me.

On the stand, your dad looked at me for a long time, then turned to the judge and said, "What my attorney said was wrong." Then firmly added, "No, your honor, she didn't do that."

The judge, impressed, said, "You're a good man."

I became a single mom. Frazzled. Overworked. Exhausted.

Mom

You did not understand things the way other people did. Your mind had its own pattern.

You, my son with the high IQ, were gifted. You could look at another person's face and know what she was feeling. When my friend came up the walk, I said, "Oh, she looks so happy."

"No," you said. "She's not happy." I took a second look. Wondering what you saw. My friend's mouth was smiling, but her suffering eyes stuck back deep in their pockets. Hollow. Mournful.

Even at play, your intelligence shone through your physical skills. Your quick hands and alert eyes moved lightning fast through the maze of Atari 1600 games on the TV screen. You and your friends, sprawled out on the floor, maneuvered the joystick while munching pizza and drinking cola chunked with ice.

You were my shopping eyes that could tell just what outfit would look best on me. It took me forever to decide because I never knew what would look right until I tried it on. The store's trail of skirts, blouses, and dresses of assorted hues and fringes dizzied me. And don't mention the shoes. I didn't have a clue.

When you walked through the mall, you could look at a rack

and imagine colors, lines, patterns, and cuts made just for me.

For yourself, Champ, you always chose the latest fashions.

You could tell which song would be a smash even before it hit the charts. I turned off Vivaldi to listen to what you were hearing from Run DMC and sat down with astonishment when you told me that Michael Jackson's *Thriller* sold more albums than the Beatles.

Sheila E. with her gorgeous drum-playing self was your dream date.

I knew you were thinking of her when you smoked cool Camels. I said, knowing you had a crush on her, "Listen, Champ. Girls don't kiss guys with tobacco breath."

You stopped smoking.

You loved Purple Rain, the concert.

You felt Prince and his Audacious Attitude with a double capital *A*.

You saw the *Purple Rain* movie over and over.

Genius is ageless. Adults who cared about their kids followed you.

You knew how to pick a winner.

You knew what you knew.

You knew what you liked.

Champ, tell me ... where did you go?

Son

"Let's go to the barbershop, Mom."

You asked, "Is it time again?"

I nodded.

You grinned.

It was one of your favorite things.

Mom

I liked to see the camaraderie among men in the barbershop. To hear the jokes. The bantering about who's got the ugliest-shaped head. The signifying. To sit down in the middle of magic-mouthed men.

I liked seeing you among them.

The barber took the towel away and shook out your clipped curly hair. Some fell on the floor, some fell in the wastebasket.

You scrutinized your image in the handheld mirror that let you check out the nape of your neck in the larger wall mirror.

"The line's not quite right," you said to the waiting barber.

He looked at you with his usual respect.

"You're the champ," he acknowledged.

He clipped the towel around your neck again and picked up his buzzing trimmer.

"Now Champ's a customer who knows what he likes," one barbershop old-timer chimed.

I liked the way the men got up to give me their seats.

Men who, I knew, had moms just like me.

They were sons, just like you.

Son

Those were better times.

"Let's go today," I told Ace the day before Prince was scheduled for the Cow Palace.

We jumped on BART, which rode us underwater beneath the Bay Bridge to San Francisco.

In the city, we boarded the Muni. Between bus transfers we joined break dancers in head spins, backspins, and picked up new moves, spinning in sizzling competition.

We passed the night camping out in sleeping bags, staking our claim early to Prince's concert at the Cow Palace. Still spinning in our minds and bodies. Me and Ace won our places among the first in line to get the best seating.

Prince opened his act, screaming lyrics from behind the curtain. "Seventeen Days." His daring voice and phat beats held us in the heartbeat of his rhythm. He shook claps from the synthesizer's keyboard.

Then the curtain swooped open. A thunderbolt, wisps of smoke and lightning, and Prince began to croon in all his ear-shattering glory. Girls in party clothes swooned, tears sparkled their makeup.

Caressing his guitar, he segued into "Purple Rain."

He drove us to a land of wildness, his writhing body, his guitar licks like white-hot flames.

"When Doves Cry" was your favorite, Mom. Maybe because
the lyrics made you hear wings flutter. Poetry.

When you picked us up, Mom, you spotted the graffiti.

"Like an outdoors gallery," you said, noticing how the pieces
and characters made canvases out of buildings, fences, and
freeway signs. Against the night sky, black-and-silver-hooded
taggers were spraying graffiti on the overhead ramps. Looked
like only other teenagers could see them.

I have pictures to remind me of even better times.

On my birthday, you took us to the arcades.

Ryan played Pac-Man, running from the ghost, then when cornered turning around and munching up his pursuer. Stevie
pushed and pulled at the Donkey Kong command post.

My fingers took flight when I played Star Gate.

Me against the machine. And I beat the machine.

A triumph on my birthday, with cheers heard all up and down the arcade, from machine to machine. Warriors roaring.

We sang an old-fashioned "Happy Birthday" at our table to please you.

But my mind was on Space Invaders and Dragon's Lair.

What a birthday. What a memory.

Although you were a quick learner, as were the other moms, I had to tell you the TV video game players to get me. You insisted I add to my own allowance if I wanted something that cost so much. Ace's mom said the same.

We could do it.

We screeched our bikes up and down the Berkeley streets. I had a Redline for my paper route. Ace pedaled a Mongoose. Ryan and Stevie, legs pumping, sped around on a Super Goose and a Schwinn Hubby.

People stuck sleepy heads out of windows when they heard the rolled up *Oakland Tribune* plop like a wake-up alarm on their front porches.

We were careful not to toss the papers into the bushes. Respectful.

These were summery days. I didn't know then how good we had it.

Maybe you knew.

You insisted on going with me to the barbershop.

You liked the sound of the men talking. Joking. And they instinctively liked you.

No, that's not all I remember, Mom.

Mom

Champ, you could eat a whole platter of hard-fried perch by yourself.

The aromas alone could fill me up. Nothing as tasty as frying catches that you and your father caught from the pier and the harbor.

You caught a whopper. You had the discipline, the method, down pat. It was on this fishing trip with your dad that he gave you your nickname "Champ."

The title took.

Oh, you looked forward to my cooking the fresh fish from the Farralone Islands spiced with peppery hot sauce. Plentiful. Neighbors dropping in. An old-fashioned fish fry.

Son

I don't know if you want to hear all this. I mean all of it.

Every time we'd drive to Lake Comanche in the mother lode country, I'd bring home a catch of trout, perch, salmon, and kingfish, you'd smile at me and say, "Thanks, Champ!"

I don't know how I caught so many wigglers, but patience and luck must have played some part.

Then maybe the joy sprinkled over everything stayed with me, too, at Half Moon Bay when I caught that magnificent salmon in the picture.

There was joy in fishing with cousins, brothers, and uncles. A male thing, with my dad at the helm.

Then dad filleted the salmon, the pink meat sweet and smelling like the bay. We headed for home and the setting sun flashed golden red.

I wanted Ace, Ryan, and Stevie to know what a wonderful time I had with my dad. And they went with us more than a time or two.

I wanted them to join us again on our next fishing trip.

Then the horror began. A jagged slash in time. An unsettling rhythm. A creased light.

I couldn't get anything right. Everything I touched, I messed up.

After the divorce, things changed drastically. But they had begun to fall apart even before the divorce. Dad missed every appointment he made with me. And he was always late.

My eyes betrayed me. I looked at something and it changed to something else before I could turn away.

The chirping of sparrows—loud squabbles.

Dad promised to take Ace, Ryan, Stevie, and me fishing at six in the morning. All of us spent the night at Ace's house. Dad didn't show up until noon.

And Ace's mom, who was also divorced and raising her sons alone, yelled and screamed at him to never show his face in her doorway again. "How dare you break a promise to your son?" she scolded. The whole neighborhood could hear her.

I was so embarrassed. You, Mom, would have called the feeling "mortified." Maybe if I had screamed, I would not have these voices stomping holes through my head, cursing me out and calling me rotten names.

Chiding monkeys hung from red oak trees that day. I was inconsolable. Boys aren't supposed to cry. I cried as my friends kept saying, "It's all right. It's all right." This was my father. And I wanted him to keep his promises.

My brain was unmending. Unraveling. How could I tell you? I didn't know why, and I didn't know where to start.

Mom, you never knew about the missed trips. The heavy, unbearable string of broken promises. The stress. You would have had ten fits. And when you got upset the disharmony in your voice hurt something fierce.

I was listening for magic in the music. A healing sound like the melody tucked inside the dove's cry.

But I pulled down songs so disturbing and out of tune that I could not weave my way back to a melody. The devils I saw and heard in this land of shadows raised their scaly wings and dulled the light.

EPILOGUE
Mom

How long did I think that it was me or your father that made you this way?

I didn't understand. So many people don't. We blame the family. We blame the patient.

"Look at that crazy sitting over there. Slobbering at the mouth." That's what most say.

But you're not alone, Champ. There are legions like you. More than anyone cares to realize.

Lackadaisical parenting, teenagers going through pimples and adolescence, fighting sisters and brothers, divorcing parents, even forgotten promises and missed appointments do not cause schizophrenia.

I understand this now, and I continue to search for knowledge.

After so many years, Champ, you're taking your medication consistently and you're keeping your appointments with your psychiatrist. You're living on your own, in your own apartment.

Triumphs.

I hope we find a cure. For you and for the millions of others. I hope we find ways to permanently mend the broken mind.

Until then I will celebrate your triumphs one by one. You finished a computer class of forty sessions at the community college and didn't miss a day. I'm proud of your victories, Champ.

Son

You took me to every doctor you could find, Mom, looking for a diagnosis.

The day you took me to Kaiser and the clinic, the answer came. Schizophrenia.

When the shape-shifting, morphing tigers stalked me, I wanted X-men and Batman, my favorite comic characters. But Batman did not fly to me.

With each step up in medication, I saw myself still standing in a circle of tigers. I just couldn't make out their eyes.

When your friend, that UCLA professor of psychology, rec-ommended one of the top psychiatrists in schizophrenia, a door opened.

He took my case and prescribed the long-awaited Clorazil. After a while I could barely make out the tigers.

Only twice in the last ten years have I not taken the new medication. You know this, Mom, during those two times the misery was beyond description. Hospitalization and pain so massive a scream can't hold it.

If there is a God of the mind, this would be my prayer: Let me look at a lamp and not see a tiger. Let me hear a moth's wings and not the clatter of a helicopter.

As you're working to help me, I help myself in every way I can.

I want to dance, Mom, with you, my family, and friends forever outside this circle of tigers.

JOYCE CAROL THOMAS

is a novelist, playwright, and poet who has taught creative writing at the University of California, Purdue University, and the University of Tennessee. Among the many awards and prizes she has received are the National Book Award, the American Book Award, and two Coretta Scott King Honor Awards. A native of Ponca City, Oklahoma, she now lives and writes full-time in Berkeley, California.

A Woman's Touch

RITA WILLIAMS-GARCIA

"**J**a-SON! JASON!"

I heard Momo calling, but I was counting on Pop's car pulling up so I wouldn't have to answer.

Sweet Pea spun his bald head in my hands. I liked the way his haircut felt. New and bristly, like a porcupine. I didn't mind my little brother being with me. He was always inching his short self under me, or Moms or Momo. He didn't care. He always found a spot to fit. That's how it is when you're small like that. You don't care, as long as you can lay your head somewhere.

"Momo calling you."

"She could call all she wanna call. Don't mean I have to jump."

I didn't look up, but I caught enough of her in my side view. Her green pants ended in boots, covered with dust from the construction site where she worked. That drove her old lady crazy when Momo clomped inside the house with all that dirt. Her mother used to rag on about being tired of sweeping dust, but that old lady never swept a floor since we moved in. My mother did that.

Sweet Pea ran to her, threading himself between her legs.

"Go on inside," she told him.

Momo's shadow hung over me.

"I know you heard me." She had been drinking coffee. I could smell it.

Yeah. So. What, what? WHAT? Sometimes I just wanna hit her. Trying to act like she my pops.

"Now I told you. The garage gotta be straight before you can go."

"Pop's coming," I said. "Any minute."

She made the humph sound, as in *don't hold your breath.* Then she came out and said it. "Look, Jason, I want to live easy and not break my back all day. You don't see me holding my breath, do you?"

Stank coffee breath. I hate her.

I turned my head to the right, the direction Pop's car would be driving up from.

"Now, Son, I already told you, you can take off with Robert, as long as that garage gets cleaned up. I'm not going to tell you again."

"Why I gotta clean it? That ain't my life story thrown around in there."

When we first moved in, I looked to Moms to keep Momo in check. Now Moms just says, "You heard her." Besides, Momo got almost a hundred pounds on me. I'm not scared of her, or nothing. But I'm just saying, she big.

"Look, Son. How'll you grow into a man, if I let you sit up in my house all summer while I break my back?"

I stood up. I was almost as tall as her.

"You can't teach me to be a man," I told her.

"Oh no?" she said. "But you *will* clean that garage."

It was her mother's fault. The old lady. Momo went crazy the day she died and threw all her stuff in the garage. She hurled piles of stuff like she was a tornado ripping through town. Just threw them. Books. Magazines. Wigs. Dresses. Shoes. Lamps. Pictures. Her walkers. Her canes. All that stuff.

Momo had stuff in the garage, too. But hers were in two boxes, both with DO NOT THROW OUT in thick Magic Marker.

I went into the garage. She was right behind me, but went inside the kitchen. The kitchen door opened into the garage. That's why the kitchen was always so cold in the morning. All that cold air sweeping in under the door.

When you're in the kitchen, you can hear everything going on in the garage, and when you're in the garage, you can hear everything in the kitchen. Moms just put some plates on the table. She waited for Momo to come in so they could eat together. Me and Sweet Pea usually ate by ourselves, unless Momo was going to be real late. Then Moms ate with us.

They're talking. It's all low and garbled. Then they laughed and Momo said, "Rub your feet? Girl, you need to rub these here."

Mom laughed the loudest. It's kinda strange to hear my mom laughing like a girl. It didn't bother me, or nothing. I've heard worse. Me and Sweet Pea's room was right next to theirs, so we heard it all. Sweet Pea cracks me up. One night he woke up and said, "Oooh, they doing the nasty." Sweet Pea didn't think it was weird. A woman and a woman. He just thought people "doing it" was funny. He was so little when we left Pop. He didn't know any better.

I still remember the night we took off, like it was yesterday. Moms had Sweet Pea in one arm, and a bag with some clothes in the other. She wouldn't let me bring my Road Racer or my trading cards. None of my stuff. She just said, "Come on," and we went to this shelter downtown. We stayed there for a while, until Momo drove up in her truck. The first time I saw her was the day we moved into this house to live with her and her mother. It was wintertime. Snowing. She kissed my moms. A man-woman kiss. Then she scooped up Sweet Pea and kissed him like he was hers. Momo knew better than to get too close to me. Anyway, when we walked inside for the first time, my mother said, "This place could sure use a woman's touch." Then they both hauled back and laughed like she said something funny.

At first I thought Momo was a man. She had a Caesar haircut like a man's, with a short slanted part shaved in the middle of her head. She even wore a stud in her ear like a man wore a stud. Not like Moms and her gold hoops. And her hands. Christ almighty. Big-assed hands. Hard and crusty. Moms did her nails. Soaked them, took out the dirt, then filed them, just like she used to do for Pop.

I looked around the garage. I didn't know where to start. All those books and photographs. Dresses. Stacks of magazines. *Jet* magazines. Cassius Clay on the cover. *Look* magazines. *Life* magazines. *McCall's.* The covers almost white. The pages all yellow and old. Bags and bags of shoes. Fake diamonds on the toes. Must have belonged to the old lady. Forget about Momo in some high heels.

Now that the old lady was gone, I can say I almost liked her. We understood each other from the time we met. "You ain't nothing to me," she said, "and I ain't nothing to you." She couldn't get rid of Sweet Pea so easily, with his punk self.

Sweet Pea called her GrandMomo and she called him Weasel. That used to crack me up.

I tried to sort everything out. I started with the books and magazines thrown all over the place. I stacked them in piles according to size. The *Jets* and *TV Guides* over here, *Look* and *Life* over there. But then almost every time I picked up a book or magazine, a snapshot would fall out, like they were bookmarks. That was all I needed. A new pile to deal with. Old photos. I picked one up. A picture of Momo and the old lady, except she wasn't all that old. Momo was in a dress and had a full head of hair. She was a kid. Like fourteen or fifteen and she was big, like she is now. It looked like they were going to church. Her mother had on a big church lady hat and wore white gloves.

I had to laugh. Momo didn't look right in that dress. In fact, she looked wrong.

I put the picture in one of Momo's boxes. I knew she didn't mean to throw that out. She had all kinds of books in that box. Old books, like *Robin Hood, Ivanhoe, Frankenstein*. Stuff like that. Big black vinyl record albums. Some little ones. 45s. A dead butterfly with its wings spread out, in a thin plastic case, like a trading card case. In the other box she had some trophies. A jump rope. A sweater. And underneath the sweater was a pair of red boxing gloves. Figures.

I left her stuff alone. I wasn't trying to learn her life story or nothing.

My mom wasn't really no dyke. She married my pops and had me and Sweet Pea. That ain't no dyke. The only reason why she's with Momo was to live in this house. Plus, Momo didn't hit her, and she gave Moms all her money after she cashed her paycheck. My mom was just playing her. I hoped Momo knew that. Her old lady knew the deal. She didn't think I heard, but I did. She said, "Francine, I didn't raise you to make a fool of yourself. She's" (my mother) "not like you. She's just here with her kids for what she can get."

A car engine rumbled and parked outside. I stopped and ran outside, but it wasn't Pop. I went back inside the garage.

It was already dark. That was okay. It was only Friday. Pop and I still had Saturday and Sunday. He was supposed to bring me back on Sunday at three, but Pop never stuck to the rules. He either brought me back too early or late. Then Moms got mad and they'd start stuff out in the yard because he wasn't allowed inside Momo's house. That didn't stop Momo with her big self from storming outside like she was gonna kick some ass. Boy, I wish she would. *KA-BLAM!* Hope she didn't think Pop wouldn't hit her 'cause she's a woman. If you gonna be all he-man flexing your muscles and stomping in work boots, you can get hit like a man.

I went back to the box to get a look at those gloves. Before I knew it, I had those gloves on and was lacing them up. A little big for my hands but I could wear them.

"Hook. Hook. Hook. Jab. Uppercut. *Unh.* One to the left. He steps right and surprises him. *KA-BLAM!* He's down on the ground." I raised my arms and shuffled. "One-two. One-two. Hah-hah. I am the heavyweight champion of the wooorld!"

Sweet Pea came out into the garage. He had one of his toy trucks underneath his arm and another in his hand.

"Jason. You be the red truck and I'll be the monster truck."

"No."

"Come on, Jason. Play monster truck with me."

"N-O. Know what that spells?"

He growled like a monster.

"Sweet Pea. Get in the house and put some shoes on."

I let him stay. Sweet Pea didn't bother me, as long as he didn't mess up my work. I kept sorting and stacking. When I looked up, he had put on a gray wig that belonged to the old lady. " 'Member this?" he said. " 'Weasel. Go bring me my teef.' "

"Take that off," I said.

"I'm pretty," he said, prancing around. He dug out the high heels with the fake diamonds and sank his feet in them. They were boats on his feet.

"Cut it out," I told him. "I gotta be done when Pop get here."

"Pop. Pop. Pop." He tried to jump, but those shoes kept his feet on the ground.

"You should be coming with me," I said.

"Momo said I don't have to go to Pop. Momo said Pop ain't coming."

Boy . . . I was burning.

I looked at my brother. GrandMomo's wig on his head. Him trying to hop around in those high heels.

The kitchen door opened and Mom stepped out into the garage. "Jason, baby . . ."

She didn't have to say the rest. That was how she said it each time: *Jason, baby. Pop can't make it this week.* That was how she walked toward me, kinda slow, to see if I needed a hug.

She took one look at Sweet Pea. "Boy, take that mess off and get inside."

Sweet Pea picked up only one of his trucks. The monster truck. "Momo right. Pop ain't coming."

As he passed by, I swerved that stupid wig off his head. I'd a snatched it off and thrown it if I didn't have those gloves on.

"Jason!" Moms said.

Then Momo came out and Sweet Pea ran to her. I was still burning, and I had her gloves on. I didn't care.

She looked around the garage to see what I had done. She nodded, like, okay, then said, "Taking a break?" She gestured to the gloves. "I can show you a few things."

Now I was sorry I had them on. I said, "You can't show me nothing."

"Jason!" Moms said.

"Those my gloves you got on," Momo said. "I can show you how to stand. How to punch."

"I already know."

"You don't say?"

"My pops showed me." That wasn't true, and it wasn't a lie either. I've seen him take a couple swings at my mother like she was a man in a ring. He swung at me, too.

She came in closer. "Humph." Another *don't hold your breath.* Momo put her big-assed hands up, flat, with her palms facing me. "Let's see what you got."

I just stood there with her gloves on.

She scooted Sweet Pea to Moms. "Come on. Let me see your stance. Let's see what Robert showed you."

Mad and foolish, I squared my shoulders and lifted my arms.

"Yeah. That's right," she said. "All right. Just tap my hands. Left. Left. Right, left, right."

Mom and Sweet Pea stood in the doorway, watching.

"Again. Left, left, right, left. right."

We did it again and again.

She swung around me and jabbed my left shoulder, light, to let me know I didn't have my guard up. "Arms getting tired?"

"Naw."

"Then hold 'em up," she said. She jabbed me again, on the right side.

My arms began to feel like lead. It was her gloves. They were sparring gloves. Not bag gloves. Bag gloves are lighter. Better for stuff like this here.

"Hold 'em up. Come on now. Hold 'em up, boy. Up. Higher. Now jab, and right, left. Jab, and right, left."

I jabbed. POW. Right in her mouth. I got her teeth. She covered her mouth with her hand. I couldn't see how bad it was until she put her hand down. Damn.

Moms and Sweet Pea came running out into the garage.

"Baby, you all right? Let me see."

"You hit my Momo. You hit my Momo." Sweet Pea was punching me, but I barely felt him.

Moms gave me a wicked eye. I've made her mad before, but she never gave me a look like she could cuss me.

Momo removed her hand. She sucked up the blood and rubbed her lip.

"It's not bad," she told my mother. "Go get me some Vaseline."

"No," Moms said. "You come in here and get cleaned up."

Momo turned my mother to the door and slapped her on the butt. "Girl, please. Just go get the Vaseline. He just got a wild punch. It ain't nothing."

"I don't like this," Moms said.

"What?" Momo said, all innocent. "It's all right. You all right?" she asked me.

I nodded.

"See. We all right."

Then Moms went back into the house and took Sweet Pea with her.

Momo sucked in some more blood, then turned to me.

"Come on, Son. Put your hands up. Let's see what you got."

RITA WILLIAMS-GARCIA

is the author of four novels for young adults and the winner of the PEN/Norma Klein Award. Her novel *Like Sisters on the Homefront* was a Coretta Scott King Honor Book and an ALA Best Book for Young Adults. Her novels *Fast Talk on a Slow Track* and *Every Time a Rainbow Dies* were also selected as ALA Best Books. She works as a manager in a marketing and media company and lives in Jamaica, New York.

Sailing Away

BY MICHAEL CART

A **crisp breeze blew** out of the north and the lake was cold, even colder than Toby had anticipated, but he forced himself to wade in anyway. *Take a breath*, he told himself sternly. *And then a step. And then a breath and then a step and breathe and step and ...*

STOP! Jesus God, it was cold! He shivered despite himself and scowled at the model sailboat tucked under his arm. Not only was he freezing to death, he also felt like a damn dork carrying a kid's toy boat. *But what the hell.* He shrugged. *What difference did it make now? Why should he care anymore what anybody thought?* And, besides, the beach was deserted this early in the spring and the lake was empty except for another solitary boat—a real one—far out on the water, its white sail a tiny cloud hugging the horizon.

Natty had loved boats.

It was Natty who'd brought him to the lake the first time. And it was Natty—or more formally Nathan, Nathan Nicholas—who had been both his best friend *and* his bête noire. Toby had found that exotic-sounding foreign phrase somewhere in his reading, but when he used it in conversation the first time—trying to impress Natty—his friend grinned his famous grin—all white teeth, twin dimples, and crinkly eye corners—and said, "Bête Noire? Who's that? A French movie star?"

• • •

They were nine the first time they came to the lake together. The water was cold that day, too. Cautious as always, Toby inched his way in like an ancient sea turtle with the gout, but Nathan recklessly galloped past him, whooping and laughing and screaming. He dove in and immediately surfaced, shooting out of the water like a playful otter, wet and sleek, his black hair plastered to his forehead. "C'mon in," he yelled.

"It's too cold," Toby, hunched over like a careworn old man, complained. If he expected sympathy or understanding, though, he got neither from Natty, who simply dove again. He surfaced—behind Toby this time—and grabbed him in a head-lock, pulling him under.

That was Natty. Everything was a baptism by fire with him.

Today the water was choppy and wading into it was like walking through memories made of molasses. Each grudging step brought back another mental image of the Nathan that had been.

Toby's oldest memory of Natty was from the first day of grade school. Little side-by-side strangers, they had been standing at the trough in the boy's bathroom when, without warning, Natty turned and peed on Toby, the warm stream of urine drenching his new trousers. Toby vividly remembered his feeling of disbelief as he stood there, as still and dumb as a statue, until Natty, laughing like a nutcase, finally finished.

That was the first time he had gotten into trouble, thanks to Natty.

Thinking Toby had peed his pants, their teacher called him a "little baby" and sent him home to his "mommy" to get clean, dry trousers.

Toby's face flushed red as he remembered that day, and suddenly the coldness of the water felt good.

He trudged in deeper.

Strangers had to be warned that the lake was dangerous because it was deceptive. It remained shallow forever, the water not rising much higher than your waist until, without warning, the bottom fell off precipitously. If you weren't prepared, you'd suddenly find yourself in over your head.

There was no way Toby could ever forget that because it had happened to him. The Nicholas family owned a summer house here, so Natty knew the lake much better than Toby did. And, not surprisingly, Natty learned to swim first, too. Even though Toby was the better student, he felt awkward around his friend because Natty's body was so much smarter. It could run faster than Toby's. It could jump higher, throw farther, and could move with such grace it seemed effortless. Natty could have been a star athlete, but he was too impatient with rules and structure to go out for sports.

He was generous with his prodigious physical gifts, though. He even taught a reluctant Toby—who was secretly afraid of the water—to swim at the lake. But he did it the hard way. He coaxed Toby, step by step, farther and farther into the water until the bottom fell away and Toby found himself six feet under.

He struggled to the surface just long enough to scream "Help!" before his body turned back into a bag of wet cement and dragged him under again.

Natty saved him, of course.

"God," Toby sputtered, "I could have drowned."

"That's why you need to know how to swim," Natty replied coolly. And then proceeded to teach him.

Even though Toby never became a particularly strong swimmer, it didn't seem to matter now. He was still waist deep in the lake. He put the model sailboat into the water and pushed it, bobbing gently, ahead of him.

The boat. It had belonged to Natty, a gift from his father. Natty used to call his dad "Saint Nicholas," because he gave him so many presents all year-round—especially after Natty's mom died.

That had been another first for Toby—his first encounter with death. The boys were ten when Mrs. Nicholas, a beautiful, dark-haired woman whom Natty resembled, died of breast cancer.

Standing next to the casket, Natty looked almost as drawn and distant as his dead mother.

"Hey," Toby said awkwardly.

"Hey," Natty replied, looking down at his shoes.

"I'm sorry," Toby mumbled.

"Me, too," Natty said and, for a terrible moment, Toby thought his friend might cry. If he did, Toby didn't know what he would do. For the first time, Natty would be the one in over his head and it would be Toby's turn to be the savior. But he didn't have a clue how to play *that* part.

Thankfully, Natty only grimaced and brightened almost immediately. "Hey," he said. "I just remembered something. C'mon." He grabbed Toby by the arm and pulled him into the next room, a kind of lounge with shabby sofas, rump-sprung easy chairs, and a dented chrome coffeepot.

On one of the chairs was the miniature sailboat. "My dad just gave it to me," Natty explained.

"Cool," Toby said.

"Someday I'm going to have a real one," Natty promised.

And so he would.

But not for another six years.

In the meantime, the toy became a talisman of the future. It sat atop Natty's dresser where he could see it morning and night, and it provided a center of play when the two boys were at the lake—the catalyst for imagined adventures on the high seas. Natty was the captain, of course, and Toby was always the first mate.

After Natty's mother died, the two were inseparable. Toby and his parents became a surrogate family for Natty. Mr. Nicholas encouraged the relationship, doubtless because he felt guilty about being away so often on business, leaving no one but the live-in housekeeper to keep Natty company. Every time his dad came home, he brought Natty a present, so predictably that Natty started calling them "St. Nicholas's guilt gifts."

Toby's folks were not so enthusiastic about the friendship, but they tolerated it because they felt sorry for Natty—well,

Toby's mom did, anyway. As for his dad, Toby more than once overheard him grumbling to his wife about things like, "What's wrong with Toby? He lets that kid lead him around by the nose."

Do I? Toby wondered. It had never occurred to him to question the relationship. The sun came up in the east. Natty was the leader. The sun went down in the west. Toby was the follower. It was the natural order of things, as simple and ordinary as breathing. Without Natty, Toby would be only half a person—and the dull half at that, the half that sleep-walked through life. It was Natty who provided the other wide-awake, vibrant half, which made Toby feel alive and complete in a way he didn't when he was alone.

At ten, Natty had been a risk taker, a universe disturber. Impatient with rules and order, he insisted on talking to Toby in class, even after their teacher had repeatedly cautioned them to be quiet.

"Stop it," Toby would hiss. "You'll get us in trouble."

"What are you afraid of?" Natty would hiss back.

"I'm not afraid," Toby would insist, shooting an uneasy glance at their teacher. But, of course, he was. And he was secretly glad when Miss Beatty finally separated them, making Natty move to a seat on the other side of the classroom.

Natty's idea of retaliation for that was to skip school the next day and go to the lake. Toby refused to go along for once and, as a result, was miserable the whole day, afraid Natty would be mad and also worried that his friend would get into serious trouble without him. But he didn't. Natty never did. Maybe it was because his father was rich; maybe it was because he was so good-looking that people wanted him to like them. Maybe it was because he never stopped to think about the consequences of his actions and so, magically, there weren't any. Whatever the reason, trouble didn't stick to him; it bounced off and stuck to Toby instead.

The first time Toby ever consciously questioned this arrangement was when they were twelve. He and Natty had gone to a carnival and Natty, bored with strolling up and down the midway and eating cotton candy, decided they should ride something called the Bullet.

"Are you crazy?" Toby demanded. Natty knew how much he hated thrill rides.

"There's nothing to be afraid of," Natty reassured him. "The ride only lasts a couple of minutes and I'll be in the car with you. Don't be such a big baby. I won't let anything happen to you. Trust me."

As always, Toby gave in.

Natty had been right about one thing: the ride lasted only a couple of minutes, but for Toby it seemed more like an hour in a torture chamber. The tiny bullet-shaped car hurtled through space at nightmare speed, spinning around and around as it catapulted to the top of an impossibly high arc and then rocketed back to Earth like a runaway elevator. It grazed the ground before it soared back into the sky, not once but repeatedly. Toby couldn't help himself; he screamed in terror, just as Natty leaned closer to shout, "Having fun yet?"

"I hate you," Toby shouted back into Natty's grinning, superior face. And for a second he did, with all his heart. It was the first time he had ever been truly, viscerally angry at his friend; and for two days after that, he didn't speak to Natty, freezing him out with an icy silence.

Until Natty apologized. "C'mon," he said, almost pleadingly, "don't be mad at me. I'm sorry. Jesus, you're like my brother. I need you."

It was the first time he had ever admitted to needing anything. And suddenly he looked so genuinely vulnerable, so forlorn, that Toby's iceberg of anger melted away and life gradually returned to normal.

Or as normal as life ever was with Natty.

Toby sighed. The lake didn't seem so cold now, or maybe he was just numb. The wind was still blowing, though, catching the sail of the toy boat and threatening to rip it from his grasp.

The only time Toby had ever been allowed to be captain, a similar wind had actually wrestled the boat from his grasp, and, lunging for it, he caused it to capsize.

"Uh-oh," Natty said ominously. "You know what that means."

"What?" Toby asked uncertainly.

"It means the captain has to go down with the ship." Natty jumped on him and pulled him down, holding him under water until Toby thought his lungs would burst.

"What are you trying to do," Toby gasped when he finally fought his way to the surface, "kill me?"

Natty just laughed. "Nah," he said. "If I did that, who would I have to persecute?" And he gave Toby an awkward, one-armed hug. "C'mon," he said, recovering the boat with an effortless sweep of his other arm, "let's go in and have lunch."

He turned toward shore and after a minute Toby—his defenses disarmed by Natty's uncharacteristically clumsy show of affection—shrugged and followed.

But he hadn't forgotten the episode. It had become one of a growing number of incidents that he remembered and puzzled over obsessively on the rare occasions when he was alone. But it was no use. Natty remained a stubborn mystery. And maybe, after all, that was the secret of his attraction for Toby.

Or maybe—just maybe—the attraction was the same kind of fatal fascination that immobilizes a mouse, frozen in its tracks by the hypnotic gaze of a hungry snake.

"That kid isn't going to be satisfied until he kills himself— or you!" Toby's dad had stormed when the pair was fifteen. He was reacting—overreacting, Toby thought—to the first really serious trouble the two boys had gotten into.

It started on a lazy summer afternoon at the lake house. Mr. Nicholas was out of town as usual, and the boys were hanging out with nothing much to do. Natty was bored— always a dangerous condition for him—and this time was no exception, since it prompted his announcement that they were going to take his dad's speedboat out for a spin. Natty was forbidden to operate the boat without an adult aboard, but such considerations had never stopped him before and they didn't stop him this time either.

It might have been okay; Natty could handle the boat under normal circumstances. But, of course, Natty didn't know the meaning of the word *normal*. So he got reckless and drove too fast and turned too sharply, and he capsized, though not before he had swamped a smaller boat.

Luckily, no one was hurt, but when Natty's dad found out what had happened, he was pissed. "They could have sued me," he grouched and then, without a backward glance, left for the airport.

Toby's dad, however, was apoplectic. "People could have been killed," he stormed and grounded Toby for two whole weeks, forbidding him to so much as lay eyes on Natty.

It was the longest period the two had ever spent apart, and Toby was surprised by how intensely he missed his friend. It was like there had been a death in the family, but there was more to it than that—there was an aching yearning or maybe even the pain of withdrawal. He had never thought of Natty as a narcotic, but now he found himself wondering if this was what an addict, forced to quit cold turkey, felt. How long could he live without Natty? How long would he *want* to live without Natty? The thought frightened and disturbed him. And so when the punishment period finally ended, and he saw Natty again, he struggled to forget it, to appear nonchalant, to act as if nothing had happened.

But it was no use. Something *had* happened, something had shifted, something had changed or was in the process of changing, like a butterfly growing inside a chrysalis. Whatever it was, it was obvious that Natty felt it, too. His eyes, looking at Toby, were different.

"You missed me, didn't you?" he asked. But it wasn't really a question.

• • •

Remembering it all these years later, Toby sighed. It was still too painful to think about.

And so, hoping for distraction, he let go of the toy boat and threw himself backward into the water, feeling its chill stab him like a knife of ice. He immediately fought back to his feet, gasping, blinking water out of his eyes and grabbing wildly for the boat, afraid, suddenly, that it had gotten away from him. But it was still there, right beside him, along with the memories, even sharper now and more intense than before.

"I missed you, too," Natty had said, looking at Toby with an intensity that was unnerving.

It was like trying to stare at the sun. Toby couldn't do it and looked away, feeling hot and cold at the same time and having trouble breathing until . . .

"Made you blush," Natty crowed. And then, like an indulgent parent with an awkward little kid, he ruffled Toby's hair.

"C'mon," he said, "let's go to the lake."

And, turning, he led the way, while Toby, in a confusion of emotions, raised his hand to touch the memory of Natty's hand on his hair.

Two months later Toby turned sixteen, and four weeks after that, it was Natty's turn.

Toby went to the lake house to celebrate with his friend.

When Natty came to the door to let Toby in, his eyes were shining as if twin searchlights had been switched on behind them.

"C'mon," he said, "you gotta see this." Grabbing Toby by

the wrist, he half dragged him through the house and out the back door and down to the lake.

And there it was.

The sailboat.

Not the model.

The real thing.

Beautiful in its newness. Dazzling in its life-size reality. The wind in its sail made it strain like a wild animal at the rope that tied it to the Nicholases' private dock.

"The guilt gift to end all guilt gifts!" Natty exulted. "C'mon," he continued, jumping into the boat. "Want to take her out?"

"Do I have a choice?" Toby smiled.

And, knowing the answer, he stepped into the boat. Natty cast off and, together, they sailed away to spend the entire rest of the day on the water. Toby had never seen Natty so exuberantly happy. He looked like he had died and gone to heaven, and Toby was glad that he had been brought along for the ride.

Everything about that day—the restless water, the tireless wind, the eternal sky with its sailboat clouds—was perfect. Absolutely perfect.

And Toby, who sensed that he was actually feeling, perhaps for the first time in his life, precisely what Natty was feeling, hoped it would never end. But, of course, it did. It had to. The sun finally started to go down; the wind picked up, and suddenly it was freezing cold.

Reluctantly they turned back to shore. And then, trying to jump onto the dock, Toby fell into the icy water.

"Shit!" he cried.

"You didn't have to do that just to amuse me." Natty grinned.

"Shut up," Toby snarled, struggling out of the water.

"Go on up to the house," Natty said. "I can finish here."

Toby didn't linger. He was freezing and he ran, almost on tiptoe, up to the house.

Unfortunately it was nearly as cold inside as out. Designed for summer use, the house was unheated except for one lone fireplace in the living room.

Toby ran for the bathroom and, stripping off his wet clothes, wrapped himself in one bath towel while he dried his hair with another.

He heard Natty come in and, when he was as dry as he was going to be, went in search of him.

He found him in the living room, building a fire.

"I need some dry clothes," Toby said.

"Let me finish this first," Natty replied.

"Well, hurry," Toby grumbled. "I'm freezing."

"Here," Natty said, "take this."

Toby took the glass his friend thrust at him. "What is it?"

"Something to warm you up. Go on; drink it."

Toby sniffed the amber liquid and made a face. "It smells awful," he protested.

"Oh, c'mon," Natty replied with mock reproof. "That's my dad's best eighteen-year-old Scotch."

Toby and Natty occasionally drank beer together and Toby had had a glass of Champagne with his parents on New Year's Eve and another on his sixteenth birthday, but he had never drunk whiskey before. He took a sip and tried not to spit it out, since it tasted as bad as it smelled. But he forced it down anyway and quickly felt as if somebody had turned up a thermostat inside him.

"Better?" Natty asked. He had a fire going now and stood up. He had an identical glass in his hand. He raised it. "A toast," he said. "To guilt gifts."

"To guilt gifts," Toby echoed solemnly; they clinked glasses and he took another cautious sip.

"Oh, c'mon," Natty chided. "There's plenty more where that came from," and he gulped down half the contents of his own glass.

Toby took another sip. And another. And then Natty, bottle in hand, was pouring more Scotch into his glass.

"Stop," Toby protested. "What are you trying to do—get me drunk?"

"Maybe." Natty grinned. Standing very close to Toby now, he was staring at him with the same unnerving intensity that Toby recognized from the time he had been grounded. And, as before, he turned away.

But this time he felt Natty's warm hands on either side of his face, turning his head around so eyes were staring into eyes and then, without a word of warning, Natty leaned forward and kissed him on the mouth.

Toby started, surprised but not really *that* surprised. Natty's lips tasted like Scotch and Toby knew he should pull away but somehow he couldn't.

He put his hands on Natty's shoulders instead, just as a chill ran up his spine on icy feet and he shivered uncontrollably.

"Still cold?" Natty asked, putting his arms around Toby and pulling him close to his ready warmth.

"Yes." Toby whispered the word even though there was no one else in the house to hear him. And then he shivered again. But this time it wasn't from the cold.

Later, when all their intensity had been urgently spent and they were lying quietly together, their bodies so intertwined in the dancing shadows from the fire that you couldn't tell where one began and the other left off, Toby felt at peace for the first time in his life. It was as if, together, he and Natty had sailed away and arrived at a previously unimaginable port that turned out to be their intended destination all along. It was a territory as comfortably familiar as their twin heartbeats, a place where they were more than friends, more than surrogate brothers, a place where they were blood.

"If you tell me tomorrow that you only did this because you were drunk, I'll kill you," Toby promised.

"Don't worry," Natty whispered in response. "I won't. I swear. Remember that time you were grounded?" he continued.

"Um-hmm," Toby replied sleepily; he could feel Natty's lips moving against his ear.

"That whole time, I lay in bed every night, looking at the sailboat on my dresser and dreaming that it was real and that you and I were on it together, sailing away someplace. I didn't know where we were going but that wasn't important. It was just you and me and nobody else. Imagining I was with you was the only way I could get to sleep."

He rested his head on Toby's chest then and was sound asleep in less than a minute.

Toby gathered his sleeping friend into his arms and, before drifting off to join him in sleep, whispered "I love you" into Natty's unhearing ear.

It was the only time he ever said it, since a week later, Natty was dead.

It was after midnight when Toby woke with a start. Someone was in his room. Standing in the shadows by his dresser.

There was a flash of lightning, followed immediately by a violent clap of thunder.

In the jagged illumination Toby recognized Natty.

"What—" Toby started to say, as Natty jerked one of the dresser drawers open and started pulling clothes out and tossing them roughly onto the bed.

"Get up," Natty ordered.

"What's going on?" Toby asked. Natty had a key to the house, and he often came in without knocking—which drove Toby's dad nuts—but never before in the middle of the night. More lightning split the darkness.

"We're going away," Natty said. And impatiently he pulled the drawer completely out of the dresser and dumped its contents onto the bed.

"Hey," Toby protested.

Natty ignored him and, going to the closet, hauled out Toby's suitcase.

"Come on, come on," he said urgently, adding it to the growing pile on the bed.

By this time, Toby was up. He grabbed Natty by an arm and swung him around so they were face-to-face.

"What's going on?" he demanded.

There was another flash of lightning. Its wild light made Natty's face look twisted like something in an old-fashioned, black-and-white horror movie.

"He's going to take the boat away from me."

"Who?" Toby asked, knowing he sounded stupid.

"My dad." And before Toby could ask why, Natty added, "I got into some trouble at the lake today. Some people said I caused an accident with the boat. They're gonna sue, I think. Assholes. Anyway, my dad went ballistic and said he was going to take my boat away from me. Well, that's what he thinks."

Brusquely Natty pulled away and turned back to the dresser. "Come on," he snapped. "Pack. We don't have a lot of time."

Toby felt like he was trapped in the kind of sweaty nightmare where terrible things keep happening but make no sense.

"Natty," he pleaded, "what are you talking about? Where are we going?"

"We're sailing away," Natty replied. "And we're never coming back. Never."

"What—on the lake?" Toby protested. "We can't do that."

"Oh, yes, we can."

Toby grabbed Natty's shoulders and looked him in the eyes.

"No, we can't. It's a *lake*, Natty. There's nowhere to sail *to*. All we could do is sail around in circles. Listen to yourself. You're talking like a little kid. C'mon, grow up."

Angrily, Natty pulled away. "Grow up?" he demanded. "Me

grow up! You're the one who's a scared little baby."

That hurt and the pain of it must have shown on Toby's face because Natty suddenly calmed down. "I'm sorry," he mumbled.

"I'm sorry, too," Toby replied, "but even if we could sail away, we can't just go. And it's not because I'm scared. It's because we're sixteen, for God's sake. We can't drop out of school to sail around on the lake forever, going no place."

"I can," Natty insisted stubbornly. "I can do anything I want."

"Then you'll have to do it alone." The words leaped out of his mouth before Toby even knew he was going to say them.

Natty gaped at him in disbelief. "I thought you were my friend," he said.

"Oh, God," Toby replied miserably. "I am, but that means I care about what happens to you—to us. That's why I say we can't go. We can't just throw our futures away."

Natty's anger came storming back. "Well, piss on you then, brother; I'll go by myself."

And he was gone. Just like that. If he slammed the bedroom door behind him, the sound was covered by the sudden clap of thunder that exploded the sky.

Toby sank down on his bed and listened to the rain cascading onto the roof.

Surely, he thought, *surely Natty wouldn't be crazy enough to try to go sailing now—with or without him.*

In the morning Toby would find him and apologize. They'd work something out. They always did.

He lay back in bed.

And then, for the second time, Toby woke up with a start

to find someone in his room. This time it was his parents who were standing by his bed.

Something had to be terribly wrong for both of them to be there.

And it was.

"There's been an accident," his father said.

"Oh, honey, I'm so sorry," his mother said. Her eyes were red. She'd been crying.

"What?" Toby demanded, even though he knew. But he had to hear it anyway.

"Natty's dead," his father said. His voice sounded dry; the words like sandpaper in his throat. "He took his sailboat out in the storm."

"What was he thinking?" his mother demanded and shook her head.

Toby's words were not an answer. They were just a keening "Oh, God, oh, God, oh, God."

Toby made the noises over and over like a chanted prayer—or a curse.

He rocked back and forth on his bed, back and forth, and refused to let his anxious parents comfort him.

All he could think was this: *the only time I ever said no to Natty, he winds up dead. If I'd sailed away with him, at least we'd still be together.*

Oh, God, oh, God, oh, God.

Later, after the funeral, a weeping Mr. Nicholas hugged Toby and told him he wanted him to have Natty's things.

"You were like his brother," the man sobbed. "You should have everything that belonged to him."

At first Toby refused politely, but when the man continued to insist, he finally admitted there was one thing he did
want. Mr. Nicholas was surprised when it turned out to be
the toy sailboat.

"Is that all you want?" He looked baffled when Toby nodded.

But it *was* all he wanted. It was all he needed. And from
the moment he lifted it down from its shrinelike position on
Natty's dresser, he knew what he was going to do.

And now he was doing it.

He'd been walking through the water more and more
slowly and now he stopped altogether. He was very close to
the precipice. He didn't want it to surprise him. He wanted
to be in control. Carefully he extended his right foot.
And then his left. And then his right. Each time his foot
touched the predictable bottom; but then, at last, his left
foot found nothing but emptiness beneath it. He pulled back
for a second to grasp the sailboat with both hands. He held
it tightly to his chest and exhaled, forcing all the buoyant air
from his body. *This time,* he thought with a grim smile, *it was
the ship that would go down with the captain.*

He stepped forward then, and both feet found the emptiness of the patiently waiting darkness.

Even through his tightly closed eyelids, the light seemed
dazzling and Toby could feel the heat of the sun warming his
body.

"C'mon, man," he heard an urgent voice pleading. "C'mon,
man, open your eyes."

Toby was confused. Where was he? What had happened? Was he dead? The only way to find out, it seemed, was to open his eyes. And so he did. He found himself looking at a white cloud floating above his head.

"Oh, thank God," the voice gasped.

Toby blinked and started to sit up.

"Careful," the voice said, and gentle hands that must have belonged to the voice pushed him back down. "You had an accident. You almost drowned. Thank God I learned CPR."

Things were slowly coming back into focus, and Toby realized the cloud wasn't a cloud after all. It was a sail. He was lying on the deck of a sailboat. And the voice belonged to a boy who was about his age or maybe a little older.

The boy looked anxious.

"How do you feel?" he asked.

"I'm okay," Toby said slowly. But was he? He took a brief inventory. Yes, he had a headache and his throat hurt like hell but he was alive after all.

"My God, you're lucky I was here," the boy said breathlessly. "I saw you go under. This lake is so goddamn dangerous. The bottom falls off so quickly."

Toby's mind was finally beginning to work. And he realized the boy thought he had gone under by accident. But there was something that Toby still didn't understand.

"Where did *you* come from?" he asked.

"I was out on the lake. Way out." The boy pointed at the distance.

And suddenly Toby remembered the tiny sail he had seen

hugging the horizon.

"But if you were so far out, how'd you see me?"

The boy blushed. And Toby noticed the binoculars hanging around his neck.

"Oh," Toby said. "I get it. You were watching me." And suddenly he understood something else about the boy who had saved his life. Something important.

"Well, it's a good thing I was," the boy said, sounding defensive. "But it wouldn't have made any difference if it hadn't been for that boat."

He nodded his head at the deck beside Toby. And there was Natty's toy sailboat.

"I never would have found you. I was too far away to see exactly where you had gone under. But that boat marked the place like a buoy. And I found you on the first dive. I guess somebody up there must like you."

Toby looked up at the sky and at the clouds hovering like sails overhead, and then he looked down and saw the same clouds reflected in the water, as if it were an enormous mirror. And all at once he realized how much this day was like the day he and Natty had first gone out on the boat.

"Yeah," he said to the boy, "I guess somebody does."

And he wondered why he had ever thought that dying would be the right way to memorialize someone who had been as vividly alive as Natty. No, he thought suddenly, that's wrong. He hadn't been trying to memorialize his friend. He had been trying to punish himself for failing his friend. But it wasn't his fault that Natty had died. In fact, Toby realized, if Natty had had his way, they would both be dead. He looked at the sailboat at his feet and sighed. Maybe Natty knew that now.

He sat up.

"Be careful," the boy said anxiously.

"I'm fine," Toby protested.

He looked at the boy who had saved him. He didn't look anything like Natty. He was stockier and he had sandy hair and freckles. And he had a nice face, kind and considerate looking, and it blushed when Toby looked at him. Toby wondered if they would be friends—maybe, in time, even family.

"I guess I should take you back to shore," the boy said.

He sounded reluctant.

Toby looked at him again. And made a decision.

"If it's okay," he said, "maybe we could sail around for a little bit, instead."

The boy grinned happily. "That would be great," he said.

"But first I've got to do something," Toby added. And he picked up Natty's boat from its informal berth beside him and set it carefully onto the water.

He watched the wind puff out the small sail and saw a wave catch it and toss it toward the distant center of the lake. He knew it would find its own way now, just as he knew he would find his.

He took a deep breath and turned away. "Okay," he said. "I'm ready. Let's go."

The new boy smiled at him. "Aye, Captain." He grinned, giving Toby a cheerful mock salute and together, then, they sailed away.

MICHAEL CART

is a past president of the Young Adult Library Services Association and former director of the Beverly Hills, California, Public Library. His young adult novel, *My Father's Scar*, and his anthologies, *Tomorrowland* and *Love and Sex*, were all selected as ALA Best Books for Young Adults. He lives in Chico, California.

Dr. Jekyll and Sister Hyde

BY SONYA SONES

THE ONLY ROOM WITH A LOCK

Lucy's chasing me down the hall again,
like a fire-breathing dragon,
hands clawing the air at my back,
calling me words
I've never even heard before.

I'm swallowing a scream,
racing through my bedroom
toward my bathroom door,
shoving it open,
ducking inside,

slamming it hard behind me,
and fumbling at the lock
with stuttering fingers,
till I somehow manage
to snap it into place.

Now I'm leaning against the door,
while Lucy slams her fists
into the other side,
my heart fluttering in my throat
like a trapped bird.

I'm sliding down onto the cold tiles
and reaching behind the hamper
to find the book that I keep hidden there

for whenever she has me cornered like this,
wondering how soon our parents will get home.

She never hits me in front of *them*.

IF *I* HAD A LITTLE SISTER

I'd French braid her hair for her.
I'd show her how to shave her legs.
And how to put on mascara
without smudging it.

I'd teach her how to dance.
And how to talk to boys.
And I'd answer
all her questions about sex.

I'd let her borrow
my Kate Spade purse.
I'd even let her hang
with me and my friends.

If I had a little sister,
I'd never call her
a stupid little selfish bitch,
or any of those other things.

And I'd never *ever* beat her up.

IT'S NOT EASY BEING ME

Living under the same roof
for fourteen long years
with the world's most evil sister.
When she isn't busy pulverizing me,
she's screaming things so hideous
that I can't even repeat them here.

But I *don't* want pity.
That's why I never
complain to my friends about her.
I can't stand that
"oh, Sasha, you poor thing" stuff.
I'm lots of things, but I am *not* a *poor* thing.

Besides.
My life could be worse.
I haven't been sexually molested.
I'm not battling leukemia.
My legs haven't been blown off by a land mine.
I don't even have athlete's foot.

True,
I have to live with Lucy.
But in seven hundred and thirty-nine days
she'll be going off to college.
I can tough it out till then.
I think.

IF I FOCUS ON HER *GOOD* SIDE

Lucy *does* have a good side.
She's got a side so good that she
even volunteers at Saint John's Hospital
every Tuesday afternoon
to hold the babies born with AIDS.

And she doesn't do it
because of how it will look
on her college applications.
I can tell by the light that's in her eyes
when she comes home, afterwards.

It's the same light that's there
on Thursday nights,
after she's been out delivering
Meals-on-Wheels.
Yup. She does that, too.

And she's even nice to *me*, sometimes.
But I try to keep my guard up.
Because it can all change
in a blink.
And it usually does.

She'll do things like spend hours and hours
knitting me an amazing sweater for Christmas,
but then get mad at me

and unravel the whole thing
before I ever have a chance to wear it.

Or she'll treat me to a movie,
and even buy me popcorn,
but then refuse to sit next to me
because she says
I'm eating it too loud.

When she's being nice,
she's so nice, nicer than nice,
that I get mesmerized into trusting her,
into thinking that she'll never be awful again—
and then she puts my headlights out.

It's like living with Dr. Jekyll and Sister Hyde.

TAKE THIS MORNING, FOR INSTANCE

Lucy's just finished
whipping me up a batch
of her killer (no pun intended)
blueberry pancakes.

She even peeled an orange for me,
and sliced it into sideways wheels,
the way she knows I like it.
And now she's sitting down
across from me in the breakfast nook,
asking me all about my new boyfriend, Peter.

How did we meet? she wants to know.
Was it a love-at-first-sight kind of thing?
Or did it just sort of creep up on me?
And she wants to know what it is about him
that I like so much.
And *exactly* how far we've gone.

And now she's telling me about *her* boyfriend,
this senior named Scott
who she's completely flipped over.
How even though they've been together for four months,
she still practically stops breathing
every time she sees him in the hall.

She tells me that she can't sleep at night because

she's so worried about what's going to happen
next year when Scott goes off to college.
And that she just hates the way
Mom's so unbelievably Dark Ages
when it comes to sex before marriage.

And sitting here with her,
sharing our secrets like this,
almost feels like sisters are supposed to feel.
Except for the fear—
hovering around the edges
of our conversation like a jittery ghost.

The fear
that somehow I'll *do* something wrong
or *say* something wrong—
and make it all disappear.

WHOOPS

Lucy's on another rampage.
And her shrieks are breaking the sound barrier.
But in spite of the racket she's making,
I can still hear my parents' knees
knocking together.

And, as usual,
they're not even *trying* to stop her.
They're just shaking their heads
and whispering,
"Your sister's so high-strung."

High-strung, my butt.
It wouldn't surprise me in the least
if years from now
my parents end up being interviewed
on the *CBS Evening News*.

They'll be talking about
how they just can't believe
that their own little Lucy
could shoot her husband and her kids,
and then kill her*self*—

I'm just glad Dad doesn't keep a gun in the house.

WOULD ANYONE CARE FOR ANOTHER SLICE OF SILENCE?

The four of us
are sitting here at the kitchen table
eating dinner.

The mom. The dad.
And the two kids.
The perfect nuclear family.

I haven't got any stepparents,
or stepsiblings,
or half brothers or sisters.

But it *feels* like
I've got a half father, a half mother,
a half life.

Maybe I'm not
the product of a broken home,
but my home is definitely broken.

LUCY'S NOT EXAGGERATING

When she says
that she's hated me
since the day I was born.

Because I was a preemie.
Which means I popped out of Mom
a whole lot earlier than expected.

And I almost died a couple of times.
So Mom and Dad spent every waking minute
at the hospital those first three months.

I can just picture
the adorable little
two-and-a-half-year-old Lucy

sitting at home, week after week,
alone with the baby-sitter,
seething.

Legend has it that she actually
threw me into the trash
the day after I got home from the hospital,

that Mom woke up from a nap
and found me wailing
in the wastebasket.

Apparently
Lucy tried to convince her
that I'd climbed into it by myself.

AND SPEAKING OF CLIMBING
INTO THINGS

I wish I could climb
into Peter's lap.
Right now.
Right *here*.

I'm sitting with him at the Coffee Bean,
sipping an ice-blended,
admiring the way his sandy hair
keeps falling across his face when he talks.

We've been together for two months already,
but every time I look at him,
the same sweet electricity
runs all through me.

And when the sun pours into his eyes and
lights them up from the inside like that,
it's like looking into water.
I want to dive in.

Dive right in
to that sapphire sea
and never set foot
on shore again.

WHEN THE TELEPHONE RINGS

I try to grab it before Lucy does,
which is hard,
since she practically keeps it
handcuffed to her wrist.

And if it's Peter,
she pretends to be me,
which *isn't* hard,
since our voices sound exactly the same.

She says things like:
"Get your buns over here, Pecker.
I want to model my new thong for you."
And even worse.

The first time she tried it,
he was completely fooled.
Until my adrenaline kicked in and I somehow
managed to pry the phone out of Lucy's talons.

But what *really* steams me
is that *now* Peter's decided that she's funny,
so whenever he calls and Lucy answers,
he eggs her on.

And then
she starts doing

her famous
Marilyn Monroe impression.

And when she does that,
I don't even stop to think.
I go for her jugular.
But Lucy just swats me away.

Like a gnat.

IN CASE YOU'RE WONDERING WHY I GO BONKERS WHEN LUCY TALKS TO PETER ON THE PHONE

It's because
she already stole
the only other boyfriend I ever had.

Even though
she knew I was
totally in love with him.

She just kept on
batting those lashes of hers
at him

and rubbing up against him
until she finally got him
to dump *me* and go with *her*.

"Can *I* help it
if Adam is attracted
to older women?" she said.

Then, a week later, she dropped him.
She never wanted him in the first place.
She just didn't want *me* to have him.

AND ADAM ISN'T THE *ONLY* THING SHE'S STOLEN FROM ME

My ladybug earrings.
My Homer Simpson key chain.
My autographed photo of Kobe Bryant.
Gone.

And my sunglasses.
The ones that Rosie brought me
all the way from Paris.
Au revoir.

But there's a black-and-blue
price to be paid
for asking Lucy
to give my things back.

So I never mentioned
the sudden disappearance of John Patrick,
my favorite stuffed bear
from when I was little.

I never even asked her
what happened to
the heart-shaped stone
that Adam gave me.

All of it's gone.

Gone.
Gone.
Gone.

But *not* forgotten.

AND I'LL NEVER FORGET

What happened
the only time Lucy ever caught me
searching her room:

I woke up
in the hospital
with my arm broken in three places.

Mom said,
"You poor kid.
Lucy told us what happened."

Dad said, "Yeah. I already nailed
that carpet down to the top step.
You'll never get your toe caught in it again."

Lucy said,
"Can I be the first one
to autograph your cast?"

And I said—
nothing.

I MEAN, WHAT WOULD HAVE BEEN THE POINT?

If I'd told them she tripped me,
they never would have believed it.
And to be honest,
I wouldn't have blamed them.

It's not just because
Lucy's got these huge brown eyes
that make her look
ten times more innocent than Bambi.

It's because
she's such a great actress.
She can turn on the tears at will.
We're talking buckets here.

So whenever I try to tell my parents
about something hideous that she's done to me,
"high-strung" Lucy just gives another one of her
Oscar-winning performances.

She turns the whole thing around
and convinces them
that it was *me*
who did the hideous thing to *her*.

She's so good at playing the victim,
that even *I* feel sorry for her
when she does it.
How sick is *that?*

VERY SICK

So whenever I can,
I get away from my family
and chill over here,
at Peter's.

Technically speaking,
his family's way screwed up.

Because after Peter's mom died,
his father got remarried
to a woman who'd been divorced twice.
But when her second ex-husband died,
she inherited *his* stepson,
plus she had her own son and a stepdaughter
from her *first* marriage.

And then, after a couple of years,
the second wife ran off with her physical trainer
and left all the kids with Peter's dad.
So he married wife number three,
who actually turned out to be pretty neat.
And she had a daughter from her *first* marriage
and then Peter's father had a baby with *her*,
plus they adopted this refugee kid from Afghanistan.

Peter says it turns out that
one of his stepbrothers

is his half sister's uncle
and that his stepsister Alice
is also his second cousin once removed.
Or something like that.

It's completely nuts.
But I love being over here.

There's always the sound of someone
practicing a clarinet or a flute.
Or sometimes you can hear duets.

There's always a couple of kids
bouncing on the trampoline in the yard.
There's always a few shooting hoops.
There's always somebody around
who can tell you a really bad joke.

Whenever I'm over here,
I can't help thinking that it's like
his family's been sewn together
out of all these random scraps
that somehow fit together perfectly
to make a beautiful patchwork quilt.

AT DUTTON'S BOOKSTORE

Peter just brought me over here
to buy me a book called *Speak*.
Even though it's not my birthday.
Or even our anniversary.

He just said he knew
I'd been lusting after it.
And he wanted me
to have it.

Now we're waiting in line to pay.
He's coming up behind me,
wrapping his arms around my waist,
and pulling me back to lean against him.

I can feel
the effect I'm having on him.
I can feel
the warmth of his breath on my neck.

I'm trying to act casual,
but I can hardly keep myself
from slipping around to face him
and pressing my lips to his.

I squeeze my eyes closed for a second
and when I open them
they fall on a book, lying on the counter
next to the cash register.

On the cover,
in these curly-swirly letters, it says:
"Sisters Understand Each Other
Because They Share the Same Roots."

Gag me.
Lucy and I may share the same roots,
but we *don't* understand each other.
And there's no way we'll be sharing

Peter.

SUPPOSE

You're lying on the couch,
minding your own business,
reading an amazing book
that the love of your life
just bought for you.

Suppose
you've been sprawled there all afternoon,
basking in the glow of his generosity,
totally immersed in the story,
loving every word on every page.

And suppose
you're just getting
to this really intense part
where you're about to find out
if Melinda gets raped or not,

when the front door
crashes open,
your sister plunges into the room,
and snatches the book
right out of your hands,

saying, "What's this? *Speak?*
Hey, I've heard this is great."
And then suppose

she heads out of the room
with *your* book in *her* clutches.

And you leap up,
shouting, "Give it back!"
And you try to grab it away
while your sister scrawls something
on the title page, fast.

And suppose
she whirls around then, and says,
"You want it? Here."
And smacks it
against the side of your head.

So hard that you have a sort of
internal rolling blackout.
Then she just pops it into your hands,
with a crooked little smile,
and saunters out of the room.

Suppose
you lurch down the hall,
still dazed from the blow,
to tell your mother
what just happened.

But, as usual,
your sister times it perfectly,
smashing into the room right behind you,
with tears streaming down her face,
and a smudge of lipstick on her cheek,

which she somehow manages
to convince your mother is a bruise,
the result of being belted by *you*,
when she refused to let you steal her book.
Her book?!

Suppose you say,
"But that's *my* book, Mom.
Peter gave it to me."
But your sister whips it open
and shows her the inscription:

"To Lucy, love Scott,"
scribbled across the title page.
Suppose your mother turns away from you then,
saying, "Sasha, I'm disgusted with you."
And wraps her arms around your sister.

What would you do then?

I'M GOING TO GET THAT BOOK BACK

Not that I'm superstitious or anything,
but Lucy *did* steal
the heart-shaped stone that Adam gave me,
right before she stole Adam.

Now she's stolen *Speak*.
What if she's getting tired of Scott?
What if she's getting ready
to steal Peter?

What if Lucy stealing *Speak*
is like some kind of sign or something?
I've *got* to get that book back.
No matter what.

I'm going to sneak into Lucy's room
and get that book back.
If it's the last thing I do.
And it *might* be.

If she catches me.

I'M FEELING FINE, *TODAY*

But I wouldn't be at all surprised
if on Tuesday afternoon,
just as I'm heading into my last class,
I'll suddenly be hit by the worst migraine
in the history of headaches.

And if I don't go home
and put some ice on it
right away,
well, there's no telling
what might happen.

Of course,
Mom won't be there
to nurse me back to health because
she'll be playing tennis with her friend Myra,
like she does every Tuesday afternoon,

and Lucy
will be going over
to Saint John's Hospital
straight after school to hold the babies
till at least four o'clock.

But I'll manage on my own.

Somehow.

IT'S TUESDAY AFTERNOON

That means Lucy's
holding her babies.
And *I'm*
holding my breath.

Because I've just ignored
the KEEP OUT OR ELSE sign
posted on her bedroom door
and I'm about to begin searching for my book.

Lucy won't be home
for three quarters of an hour,
but my heart
refuses to believe that,

and my arm's throbbing
in three places
with the memory of what happened
the last time I was stupid enough

to try something like this.

WHERE *IS* IT?

It's not in her closet.
Not hidden under all the junk
that's crammed into her dresser.
Not behind the cushions on her window seat.

Not *anywhere*.

Not in her nightstand drawer.
Not under the dirty clothes
in her laundry basket.
Not behind her TV.

Where *is* it?

Not in her guitar case.
Not behind her desk.
Not under her bookcase.
Not behind her computer.

It's *got* to be here somewhere.

It's not stashed under her bed
or under her pillow
or jammed between
her mattress and her box spring.

Time's running out.

It's almost four thirty.
Lucy'll be home any minute now.
Come on, *Speak*, speak to me.
Tell me where you *are*.

HEY, WAIT A MINUTE

I forgot to check in Lucy's bathroom.
She likes to read in the tub.

Maybe she didn't even
bother to hide it.

Maybe she figured I'd never dare
search her room for it, anyhow.

Maybe she just left it lying right there
next to the tub.

I bet that's exactly what she did.
Why didn't I think of this sooner?

I grab the handle of her bathroom door
and push it open—

a sudden sloshing, a splashing,
a gasp,
a stifled scream—
What the—?!

Someone's in the bathtub—
It's Lucy!

Lucy.
And Scott.

SUDDENLY

The only sound in the room
is of the clock
on the shelf above Lucy's sink,
ticking off the seconds
in painfully slow motion.

Lucy and Scott
are staring at me,
wide-eyed,
up to their necks in bubbles.
And I'm staring back.

I'm just standing here in the doorway,
staring at Lucy and Scott staring at me,
listening to the seconds tick by,
trying to get my mouth to speak,
trying to get my feet to run,

when the noise of the clock is suddenly
drowned out by another sound,
the sound of my mother's voice,
calling, "Loooooseeee . . ."
And a second later Mom's standing right there—

at Lucy's bedroom door.

MOM SEES ME

Standing here
in the bathroom doorway,
but she can't see
the bathtub
from where she is.

"Have you seen Lucy?" she asks.
"Lucy?" I say,
staring right at my sister,
who's staring back at me with a look in her eyes
that I'm sure I've never seen before.

"Lucy?" I say again,
raising one eyebrow,
and letting a crooked little smile
spread slowly across my face,
while I stare straight at my sister,

who's sitting there,
naked,
right next to naked Scott,
with Mom standing
only ten feet away.

Tick.
Tick.
Tick.

Tick.
Tick.

I savor the sound
of time passing in slow motion,
and then I hear myself saying,
"Did you forget, Mom? This is Tuesday.
She's over at Saint John's holding babies."

AT LEAST I *THINK* IT
WAS ME WHO SAID IT

I mean,
it *must* have been me.

But, do me a favor.
Don't ask me why I did it.

Because I haven't
got a clue.

WHEN I GET BACK FROM THE LIBRARY

Which is where I made Mom take me
so that Scott would have enough time
to sneak out of Lucy's bedroom
without getting caught,

I guess I'm sort of hoping for
something along the lines of a smile
or maybe even a thank-you from Lucy.
But as soon as Mom isn't looking,

she forces me down the basement steps
and corners me next to the furnace,
demanding to know exactly what I was doing
in her room this afternoon.

My heart's threatening
to leap right out of my chest,
but I take a deep breath,
and say, "I was trying to find my book."

For a second she looks like she's
contemplating which of my legs to break first,
but she just says, "I thought so,"
and hands me my copy of *Speak*.

Then she turns,
and heads back up the stairs.

A FEW MINUTES LATER

I walk
into my bedroom,
and switch on the light.

There
they all are,
lined up neatly on my bed:

my ladybug earrings,
my Homer Simpson key chain,
my sunglasses,

my autographed photo of Kobe Bryant,
the heart-shaped stone
that Adam gave me,

and even John Patrick,
my favorite stuffed bear
from when I was little.

Whoa.

JUST THINK

If Mom's friend Myra
hadn't eaten that bad shrimp at lunch,
then she wouldn't have thrown up
and the tennis game
wouldn't have been cut short
and Mom wouldn't have gotten home early
and I wouldn't have had to cover for Lucy
and Lucy wouldn't have been
incredibly grateful to me
for saving her skin
and I wouldn't have been reunited
with John Patrick
or any of my other stuff.

The moral of the story?
Sometimes bad shrimp is good.

IT'S BEEN NINE DAYS NOW

And Lucy hasn't screamed at me once.
She hasn't taken anything of mine.
She hasn't even hit me.
But she sure has looked like she *wanted* to,
a couple of times.

And when Peter calls,
she just passes the phone over to me
without even talking to him,
though she *does* plant
a big, wet, *noisy* kiss on it first.

I don't know how long this will last.
But I seriously doubt it's permanent.
So I'm finally going to do something
that I should have done
as soon as I was old enough to walk:

I'm signing up for karate.

SONYA SONES

is the author of two novels in verse: *Stop Pretending* and *What My Mother Doesn't Know*. *Stop Pretending* won both the Claudia Lewis Poetry Award and the Myra Cohn Livingston Award in Poetry; it was also a finalist for the *Los Angeles Times Book Prize*. *What My Mother Doesn't Know* was an ALA Best Book for Young Adults and a Top Ten Quick Pick. She lives with her family in Santa Monica, California.

Snowbound

BY LOIS LOWRY

The December weekend that Evelyn Collier, age eighteen, came home from college in order to introduce her boyfriend to her family was the same weekend that it had begun to snow on Friday morning. On Friday evening, when the travelers arrived, it was still snowing.

Mrs. Collier, inquiring about their luggage when the pair stood stamping snow from their shoes in the kitchen, was informed by her daughter that there was none.

"No suitcases?" Mrs. Collier asked, shivering as she pulled the kitchen door closed and peered through its window toward the dented, rusty car in which her daughter had just been transported one hundred miles through increasingly heavy snow by a young man who was not wearing a coat.

"We're into minimalism," Evelyn explained to her mother.

"Not even, ah, toiletries?" Mrs. Collier asked, aware even as she raised the question that toiletries and minimalism were probably mutually exclusive concepts. In addition, looking more closely at Evelyn and her still-to-be-introduced friend and sniffing surreptitiously, Mrs. Collier realized that neither her daughter nor the bearded boy had used comb, shampoo, or deodorant for an extended period of time.

Toothbrush? Mrs. Collier found herself wondering, but decided not to ask. She willed herself not to think about the possibility of clean underwear, either.

Mr. Collier, who had closed his law office early because of the storm, entered the kitchen to greet his much-loved only daughter, whom he had not seen since Thanksgiving. At Thanksgiving Evelyn had still combed her hair and worn nail polish.

"This is Loosh," Evelyn said cheerfully to her parents, and she gestured toward the boy, who grunted.

Loosh. Mrs. Collier remembered that the boy's name, conveyed the previous week in an airy phone call from her daughter, was Lucien something. She smiled politely at him, realizing as she did that although most of the moisture in his straggly dark beard was probably melting snow, he also had a very runny nose. As she watched, he wiped it with the sleeve of his shirt. She noticed acne under the thinnest spots of his facial hair. And there was, she saw with dismay, a crumpled pack of Marlboros in his breast pocket.

The youngest Collier, Evelyn's brother Kirby, who was eight, had been staring at the pair with his mouth open, exposing new large teeth which were slightly overlapping and would probably need orthodontia. Evelyn's teeth had cost the Colliers three thousand dollars, Mrs. Collier remembered suddenly; they were straight, even, small, and white. But now her daughter was a minimalist and did not travel with a toothbrush. Mrs. Collier had a sudden, fierce impulse to howl with grief.

"I have to start with a seven-letter word and get to another seven-letter word in six steps," Kirby explained, holding up a pad of yellow legal paper. "You change one letter each step. I'm starting with *crushed* as my seven-letter word."

"*Brushed,*" his mother, still thinking about her daughter's teeth, said firmly. "Change the *C* to a *B* and use *brushed* as your next step."

"Okay." Kirby, ever cheerful, closed his mouth over his protruding central incisors, leaned over the pad, and carefully printed the word *BRUSHED* below CRUSHED in uppercase letters.

"We have to read a really boring poem over the weekend," John announced, entering the kitchen with a textbook in one hand and a glass of chocolate milk in the other. The Colliers' older son, John, was fourteen, a ninth grader surprised by nothing. He barely glanced at his newly arrived sister or her grunting companion. "It's called 'Snowbound.'"

Lucien spoke for the first time. "Whittier sucks," he said.

Evelyn's father, standing in the kitchen with a newspaper in his hand, had seemingly been struck mute. Now he took a deep breath. "Lucien," he announced to the bearded guest, "you'll be sleeping in the family room. Come help me open up the couch."

"I don't think he's wearing any underwear," Mr. Collier said tersely to his wife when they were briefly alone in the kitchen before dinner. "When he leaned over to help with the couch, his shirt and pants parted company and there was no visible evidence of underwear."

"You sound like a lawyer. Visible evidence."

"I *am* a lawyer," Mr. Collier pointed out. "What about Evelyn? Is *she* wearing underwear? Am I paying thirty-two thousand a year for a college that teaches them to discard their underwear?"

Mrs. Collier sighed and began stirring ingredients into a large pasta salad. She had planned on lasagna for dinner. She had made a large lasagna, Evelyn's favorite, in honor of her daughter's visit. Now the menu had changed.

"You know why I'm making pasta salad—normally a warm-weather dish—on a cold, snowy night?" she asked her husband resentfully. "Pasta salad with a lot of vegetables in it?"

He raised an eyebrow. "Why?"

"Evelyn told me they don't eat mammal."

Mr. Collier looked confused. "They don't do what? Who is *they*?"

"*They* is Evelyn and that boy. Loosh? Is that what she calls him?"

"Loosh," her husband repeated in a mournful, puzzled tone.

"Right. Well, Loosh and Evelyn are vegetarians of a sort. They do not eat mammal. That's the way she said it: *mammal*. Not mammals."

Mr. Collier sifted through his memory of what constituted mammal. "Chicken? They would eat chicken, I think."

His wife stirred the salad forcefully. "Unfortunately I do not have any chicken on hand. I have a very large lasagna, the sauce of which is filled with sautéed mammal.

"I'd like to throw it at her," she added.

"It's still snowing," Kirby pointed out cheerfully at dinner. "The guy on the weather channel said 'No End in Sight.'"

John had brought his school poetry textbook to the kitchen table and was hunched over, reading, as he ate. Ordinarily Mrs. Collier would not have allowed that. But it was no longer an ordinary dinner. It was a dinner without mammal.

"We each have to memorize two lines. That's called a couplet, in case you didn't know. I haven't chosen my couplet yet. They're all boring." He read, in a dramatic, exaggerated voice, two lines from the Whittier poem:

"Unwarmed by any sunset light
The gray day darkened into night, . . ."

Outside the kitchen, the wind howled. Mr. Collier rose, took his empty plate to the sink, and stood looking through the window at the storm. "I think I'll build a fire in the fireplace," he said. "I wouldn't be surprised if we lose our electricity." He turned and went to the family room; they could hear muffled thumps as he arranged the logs and the scratch of one of the large matches they used to light fires.

"Hey, Loosh," Evelyn said, "won't that be way cool, to have firelight when we go to bed?"

Mrs. Collier looked at her daughter, who was still eating pasta salad. While her mother watched, Evelyn picked up one tubular piece of macaroni and slid it into her boyfriend's mouth. He licked her finger clean.

"Evelyn," Mrs. Collier said suddenly, "you are sleeping in your own room. Remember your bedroom, the one upstairs, with the yellow bedspread? Your, ah, friend here is sleeping in the family room. But you are not."

Evelyn rolled her eyes in disdain. So did the bearded boy.

Kirby had taken out his yellow pad again. He balanced it on his dinner plate and examined the printed words.

"Now I change one letter in *brushed*," he said, "and make a new word for step three."

"*Blushed*," his mother suggested, with an edge to her voice.

"Cool," Kirby said happily, and began to print.

"Way cool," Mrs. Collier replied, and finished clearing the table.

> "*Shut in from all the world without,*
> *We sat the clean-winged hearth about, . . .*"

The fire was crackling and they could hear wind resonate through the chimney. The electricity was still functioning. Mr. Collier, seated in his favorite chair in the family room, was reading the newspaper. John, cross-legged on the opened couch, now bed, looked up occasionally from his assigned poem and read a particular couplet aloud in a theatrical voice. Kirby, wearing pajamas with baseball players on them, was curled on the floor in the corner with the Lego castle he had been building for days. He walked a plastic knight around the top of the castle wall and murmured in the special formal voice he used for his medieval characters. "I shall defend this fortress with boiling oil if necessary," the shiny pale-gray knight said, and Kirby pivoted his right arm upward to aim his plastic sword toward the ceiling.

Evelyn had disappeared. So had Loosh.

"Where are the minimalists?" Mrs. Collier asked.

"I told him he couldn't smoke in here," her husband explained. "He's probably out on the back porch catching pneumonia, which will go well with his lung cancer."

"Dad," said Evelyn, emerging from the bathroom, "that's infantile. Anyway, Loosh isn't outside. He's in the bathroom."

"I thought *you* were in the bathroom. What's he doing in there with you? *Smoking?* I told him not in the house."

"No, not smoking," Evelyn replied in an exaggerated tone, as if she were explaining something rudimentary to a toddler. "Peeing."

Kirby looked up cheerfully. "That can be my step four!" he said. *"Flushed!"*

Evelyn looked at her little brother with affectionate pity. "Flushing is so unevolved," she told him.

John declaimed two more lines just as Loosh reappeared, zipping his fly.

> "We sped the time with stories old,
> Wrought puzzles out, and riddles told, . . ."

"See?" said Loosh, ostentatiously smelling his own fingers in some sort of mysterious appraisal. "What did I tell you about Whittier? Sucks."

"Well," announced Mrs. Collier to her husband as they snuggled together in bed, while the wind rattled the windows and frozen branches clinked like wind chimes outside, "I never thought it would come to this. But here's a confession. I hate my own daughter."

"No, you don't," her husband reassured her. "That isn't your daughter. That person in the yellow bedroom is an absolute stranger who just showed up to take shelter from the storm."

"Where is my daughter, then? What happened to her? I sent her off to college with a trunk full of new clothes, and she disappeared." Mrs. Collier began to cry. "I want her back," she wailed.

Her husband was not listening. At least not to her. Nor was he listening to the clink and rattle of the storm against their home.

"I have to revise my last statement," he announced after a moment.

"What?" His wife sniffed. "What are you talking about?"

"I referred to the person in the yellow bedroom," Frederick Simpson Collier, attorney-at-law, reminded her. "But I was mistaken. There is no person in the yellow bedroom. The yellow bedroom is now empty. The person who used to be our daughter just closed its door very quietly and tiptoed down the stairs to join her, ah, companion in the family room."

"Oh, God," Mrs. Collier moaned, and buried her face in her pillow.

In his own bed two rooms farther along the upstairs hall, fourteen-year-old John heard the sleet slice against the windows.

He had also heard his sister tiptoe down the stairs.

Damn, John thought, feeling inexplicably angry.

He agreed with whatever his name was that the Whittier poem sucked. Or sort of sucked, at least. It was boring and outdated and if he had to read something for English class, he would rather be reading science fiction instead of any kind of poetry.

This family is all huddled in their house, see, just the way Whittier described, and it's snowing like gangbusters outside so no one can go out; anyway, little do they know that the snow is an alien precipitation of some sort, something toxic from another planet—

He heard his parents murmuring and thought he heard a muffled sob from his mother. John paused in the sci-fi tale he was telling himself, and listened, but now the house was quiet except for the churning murmur of the furnace.

So, see, like this one person in the house is actually an alien, cleverly disguised (this other civilization has been studying Earth, see, learning earthly habits so they can infiltrate), and he (it?) has been trained to seduce a young female—

John interrupted that train of thought. He decided he wouldn't go too deeply into the seduction techniques. *Stick with the toxic snow,* he told himself, and drifted into sleep.

Kirby had been sound asleep for two hours. He didn't hear his mother weep or his father grumble or his sister move stealthily down the stairs. He didn't hear the sharp click of wind-shattered icicles snap and drop from the eaves.

He had gone to sleep hoping that the storm would continue long enough for school to be canceled on Monday but that snowplows and snowblowers would free them enough for his friend Alexander to come over. Alexander lived next door. Alexander was Special Needs. He had repeated third grade and had a tutor but could not understand or remember the multiplication tables. Still, he was cheerful, agreeable, good at construction, an enthusiastic colleague in Lego projects, and Kirby's best friend. Kirby and Alexander had been working every afternoon on the complicated Lego castle, with its turrets and battlements; soon they would get the drawbridge figured out. The entire structure was now reaching immense proportions in the corner of the family room. A snow day on Monday would mean that he and Alexander could work on the castle for uninterrupted hours.

In his deep sleep, Kirby dreamed of a fortress: of being inside, of feeling safe, of pulling up the drawbridge to keep invaders at bay.

Downstairs, in the opened sofa bed in the family room, Evelyn nudged Lucien's shoulder and whispered, "Sweetie, you're snoring."

He raised his head. "So?" he said. "I *told* you I have a fucking deviated septum.

"You're hogging the blanket," he added, yanking at it. Then his mouth fell open and his snoring resumed.

Evelyn stared at the ceiling. She was chilly without the blanket that he had yanked away, and she was nervous about trying to retrieve a portion of it. Loosh had a very bad temper.

The fire had died out several hours before. But the relentless snow made the night oddly bright, and she could see the familiar objects in the room around her: the massive Lego castle in the corner; her mother's knitting in a basket, two needles erect as antennae; the newspaper her father had left folded in his chair; and John's poetry book open to the Whittier poem on the coffee table.

Remembering her brother's diligent reading of the

tedious poem, Evelyn thought guiltily that she should be working on a paper due next Thursday in her classics course. She'd had a pretty good start on it, but Lucien had told her to knock it off because who cares about classics anyway, classics is irrelevant. And Lucien thought it plebian to study.

Of course, Evelyn mused, Lucien didn't need to. He had dropped out of school a month ago after flunking most of his midterms.

> *"Next morn we wakened with the shout*
> *of merry voices high and clear;*
> *And saw the teamsters drawing near*
> *To break the drifted highways out. . . ."*

John set the book aside and gulped down a glass of orange juice. "I didn't know they had teamsters back then," he said.

"They had *real* teamsters. Teams of oxen to clear the snow," his father explained. "We get snowplows. Listen: here it comes."

The family paused and listened to the reassuring rumble of the massive snowplow on their road. The kitchen was blindingly bright now, with full sun on the drifts outside. Mrs. Collier poured coffee for herself and her husband.

"Maybe a merry shout would dislodge that boy in the family room," she suggested.

John shook his head. "He didn't budge when I walked through to get my book. He was snoring. He still is."

They all listened, and it was true.

"Poor Loosh. He has a deviated septum," Evelyn explained

sympathetically. She had emerged fully dressed from her yellow bedroom upstairs, having magically transported herself there during the early morning hours so that she could sleep under a blanket.

"I'm up to *flushed* and I only have two more to go till I get to six," Kirby announced, and chewed on the eraser of his yellow pencil.

There was a noise from the family room. One final snorting sort of snore, followed by a cough. Then the sound of two feet planted on the floor and a loud yawn. "Jesus, that bed's hard," a voice said. Then as the Collier family watched, a blur of pale, naked, bearded flesh ambled across the hall to the bathroom.

"*Flashed,*" Mrs. Collier said to Kirby in a pained voice.

"Who's that guy?" Alexander asked. He had made his way, following the narrow path carved by his father's snowblower, from next door. Now his boots were sitting in their own puddles on the landing of the cellar stairs, and his soggy mittens were draped over a radiator.

He and Kirby were hunched over their Lego castle. Kirby had fashioned a kind of portcullis from a piece of broken garden rake. Though it was bamboo, he thought that if they painted it silver it would appear to be an iron grate. Carefully they had attached it to fishing line on either side and were trying to create a pulley system that would lift and lower it.

Kirby stood two plastic knights on a battlement overlooking the moat. "See, these guys stand up here on the wall, and when they see enemies coming—"

"Would they have binoculars?" Alexander asked. He made himself a pair of binoculars from his hands and viewed the fireplace, his mittens, and the door to the hall.

"I don't think so. But they had very good eyes then. They didn't ruin them with TV." Kirby moved a knight to the handle of the pulley and very tentatively lowered the portcullis. "Cool. It works."

"Who's that guy?" Alexander asked again. "He's picking his nose." He aimed his hand binoculars toward the kitchen. Kirby looked over and saw that Alexander was peering at his sister's boyfriend, who was at the kitchen table eating raisin bran. There were dribbles of milk in his straggly beard.

"I don't know. He's visiting. He eats with his mouth open, and sleeps naked."

"Gross," Alexander said.

"If he approaches the castle, we'll pour boiling oil on him," Kirby announced with satisfaction.

By Saturday afternoon John gave up hope that school would be canceled on Monday. The snow had stopped, the sun was shining, and the plows were out. Sprawled on the folded family room couch with the poetry book propped in front of him, he stared at the lengthy poem without reading, and half listened to the little boys discussing medieval weaponry as they moved their plastic knights and squires around.

His sister's friend, mouth open, eyes glazed, was staring at silent cartoons on the muted television. "You really need to watch this shit stoned," he complained, but no one responded.

Evelyn had disappeared upstairs with her mother.

So this alien integrates—no, insinuates—he insinuates himself successfully into an ordinary household, using the daughter as an innocent pawn; but then he louses up the whole scheme because on his own planet they had not understood anything about . . .

He left that part blank in his mind, to be filled in later.

And the stuff was toxic in other galaxies, so the alien thought it was toxic on Earth? It wasn't. Here on this planet it was really actual snow, and people shoveled it up and made snow forts and snowballs and snowmen, but the evil alien . . .

That was it: the word he'd been looking for. John went back in his mind and filled in the space he had left blank.

They had not understood anything about fun.

He tested it. "You want to go out and build a snowman?" John asked the room in general.

Kirby and Alexander both leaped to their feet. Then, conscientiously, Kirby turned to his castle and made an announcement. "Night is falling, and war will resume at dawn," he said to his knights. He leaned down and tipped them all sideways so they could sleep on the battlements, plastic legs extended. One by one he flipped their movable visors down over their molded faces.

The boy named Loosh continued to stare at the soundless TV as a toy commercial began. John cupped his fingers into a megaphone and aimed his voice toward the couch. "Earth to alien," he said loudly. "Snowman? Outside?

"Fun?" he added pointedly.

His sister's friend spoke without shifting his eyes. "I need to watch this," he said.

The little boys were already in their boots and mittens and jackets.

"Evelyn?" John called up the stairs. "You want to come out and make a snowman with us?"

"Sure," she called back happily. "I'll be right there. How about a snow woman?"

It was that subtle oversight that brought about the downfall of the evil alien; for although he had been fiendishly clever in his preparation and in the infiltration, he was not able to overcome— or even to perceive his lack of understanding of . . .

"Look at that sunshine!" Evelyn interrupted his thoughts. She rummaged in the closet for a parka. "Can I borrow one of your hats? I didn't bring one." John nodded, and watched as his sister pulled a blue ski hat down over her hair.

"Loosh? Are you coming?" she called.

When there was no reply, John explained, "He's watching cartoons." Through the window he saw the little boys, already in the yard, beginning to roll the snow into expanding balls.

"Loosh?" Evelyn called again. There was a grunt in reply, and then a creak from the couch as the boy unfolded himself and rose. They could hear him plant one bare foot and then the second on the floor.

Then they heard a crash.

"*Jesus!* What's all this crap on the floor? I walked right into it!"

Evelyn and John rushed to the doorway in time to see the boy kick viciously at what remained of their brother's structure.

"Those two little retards! They built this piece of shit right where they knew I'd be wanting to walk!" he said angrily, and kicked again. The final standing wall, carefully constructed in a red-and-white alternating pattern, toppled.

"I can't believe it," Evelyn said. "You destroyed the castle."

Mrs. Collier took the lasagna, its cheese-crusted top tan and bubbling, from the oven and placed it on the kitchen table. It was dark now, the early dark of a winter evening, and the kitchen windows were blurred with steam so that the lamppost at the end of the driveway was a soft blur of golden light.

The driveway was empty, though a patch of dark, solidified oil smeared the packed snow in the place where the rusted car had been parked the night before.

"I hope he's all right," Mrs. Collier murmured, glancing through the steamed window toward the driveway. "I keep thinking of his parents and how they must worry. He wasn't even wearing a coat. And I doubt if that car has snow tires. I thought I saw it skid a little on the ice when he pulled out into the road."

"He'll be okay," Evelyn said, and began putting folded napkins by each place at the table.

"And you? Are you okay?"

Evelyn nodded. "Dad said he'd drive me to the bus station tomorrow afternoon. And that gives me time to get some work done on my classics paper tonight."

"I meant—"

"I know what you meant. I'm fine. Embarrassed, but fine."

Evelyn's father entered the kitchen and eyed the lasagna. "I'm opening a bottle of wine," he announced with satisfaction.

John, on his knees in the family room, was helping his brother reconstruct the castle. Kirby placed a knight upright beside the partly repaired wall and straightened the plastic helmet. He stared at the wreckage and appeared to be thinking. Then he grinned.

"I got my sixth word!" Kirby announced suddenly. "Remember five was *flashed?* Well, I'm changing the *a* to an e."

"Wait, let me guess," John said.

"No, let *me* guess," Evelyn called from the kitchen.

"De-flesh," John announced. "I'm going to use it in the science fiction story I'm writing. When they catch the alien, they take tiny sharp knives, and veeerryy slowly, they de-flesh him—"

"Gross," Kirby said, giggling. "And wrong, too."

"Shelfed," Evelyn suggested. "Dad, my room in the dorm doesn't have enough bookshelves. Would you be willing to—"

"Wrong again," Kirby announced. He gathered his paper and pencil and brought them to the kitchen. "Look," he said, and wrote his sixth set of letters at the end of the column. Carefully he added an apostrophe.

"It's not really one word," he said, staring at it. He held up the paper. "But I don't think it matters."

"'He's fled,'" Kirby read aloud.

"He's fled," John repeated, and pictured the alien returning to his planet on a spaceship with bald tires and no heater.

"He's fled," Mr. and Mrs. Collier said together, smiling slightly at each other.

"He's fled," Evelyn said. "Do me a favor, and let's never talk about this?"

John picked up his poetry book, still open to Whittier.

"Wide swung again our ice-locked door,
And all the world was ours once more!"

"Let's eat," Mrs. Collier said, and began to serve mammal to her family.

LOIS LOWRY

is a two-time winner of the Newbery Medal for *Number the Stars* and *The Giver*. A former journalist and photographer, she is the author of more than twenty-five books, including the celebrated Anastasia Krupnik series. She divides her time between Massachusetts and an 1840s farmhouse in rural New Hampshire.